C29 0000 1219 772

D1421534

LIVING IN THE DARK

A mysterious phone call from a man in a phone booth re-opens a thirty-year-old unsolved murder case — but the investigation takes an awkward turn when the evidence begins to point to a retired policeman . . . DI Casey Clunes's teenage babysitter mysteriously goes missing, and her husband Dom is suspected of being involved . . . And when evidence of an old murder begins to come to light, the culprit takes some desperate measures to warn people away. DC Laura Malone is on the case — but is she next in the murderer's sights?

GERALDINE RYAN

LIVING IN THE DARK
& Other Stories

Complete and Unabridged

LINFORD
Leicester

First published in Great Britain

First Linford Edition
published 2018

A catalogue record for this book is available
from the British Library.

ISBN 978–1–4448–3949–4

Published by
F. A. Thorpe (Publishing)
Anstey, Leicestershire

Set by Words & Graphics Ltd.
Anstey, Leicestershire
Printed and bound in Great Britain by
T. J. International Ltd., Padstow, Cornwall

This book is printed on acid-free paper

LIVING IN THE DARK

FEBRUARY 1958

It was nearly five o'clock, and tea would be in an hour. But Luke had stayed for football practice after school, and he was starving and knew he wouldn't be able to wait that long. Propping his bike against the shop wall, he pushed open the door of the newsagent's. After the biting cold of the February evening, the shop was a welcome warm refuge.

There was quite a queue at the counter, so he resigned himself to waiting. He passed the time studying the chocolate bar display and imagining what he'd buy if he had half a crown to spend instead of the measly sixpence Ruth had given him for not dobbing her in to Mum and Dad. He'd asked for a shilling at first but she'd just laughed in his face. Still, sixpence was better than nothing, he supposed.

Mrs Riley behind the counter was usually very smiley, but tonight she was quieter than usual, exchanging hushed words with each customer as she gave them back their change. It was a bit like being in church on a Sunday morning, Luke thought. Or like that moment before sir said please turn over your paper when they did exams. He just wished everybody would get a move on.

He fished in his pocket for his money so he could have it ready to put into Mrs Riley's hand and selected a Mars bar from the display. Ideally he liked them cold, because then they were nice and chewy and lasted longer. His best friend Gary had a fridge because his dad worked for English Electric, and he was allowed to stash all his chocolate inside it in the summer. Luke had asked Mum when they could get one, but she'd just laughed. He decided this laughing at perfectly sensible suggestions had to be a female thing.

There were only two people in front of him now. A glance at the clock on the wall showed him it was a couple of minutes off five. His gaze fell upon the pile of newspapers stacked on the counter, and he cast his eye over the headlines.

UNITED DISASTER, he read. GRIM FIGHT FOR LIFE. Underneath there was a photograph of the Manchester United football team lined up in two rows, arms folded and smiling for the camera. And another picture next to it. Fuzzy. A smouldering wreckage, shrouded in smoke. People standing about, at a loss what to do.

'Tragic,' the woman in front of him said. 'All those lives lost. Some of them are just boys.'

'They say it's touch and go if Duncan Edwards will survive too,' someone else said.

Luke felt sick. It was as if all his bones were suddenly melting and if he didn't get out of the shop right now he might fall over. He spun round and made a dash for the door, ignoring Mrs Riley's agitated cry of 'Oi, you!' as he let it slam shut behind him.

Once outside, he jumped on his bike. Pointing it in the direction of home, he pedalled furiously, wishing he could get that photo of the wrecked plane out of his head.

They couldn't all be dead; it wasn't possible. Only yesterday they'd drawn with Red Star Belgrade. That meant they'd won on aggregate! They'd been on their way home to celebrate their victory. But then this had happened.

It was when he transferred his Mars bar from one hand to the other in order to signal that it hit him for the first time. He'd left without paying for it. He was in possession of stolen chocolate. He was going to be in so much trouble for this! Could he turn round and take it back? He certainly didn't feel like eating it, not now.

There was a police car standing outside his house. They'd come for him! Mrs Riley must have called 999. She knew his name and where he lived, because that was where Mum and Dad got their papers from. Oh, God. He was in trouble now. With a heavy heart, he dismounted from his bike and wheeled it up the path.

FEBRUARY 1988

He'd made a bargain with himself. If the next phone he came to wasn't working, then he'd go home and try again the next morning. He was drunk, but with drunkenness had arrived a brilliant clarity. He wasn't afraid anymore. He was going to die anyway. He was a ticking time bomb, the doctor had told him. So what did he have to lose?

The night was silent. Occasionally from the distance came the muffled sound of a passing car. The pubs had long since closed, and no one with any sense would be out on a night like this. His footsteps, almost deadened by the fog, and his jagged breathing were his only companions.

He was so deep in his thoughts that he nearly walked past it. The phone box loomed up out of the foggy night, an abandoned pile at the side of the road. He went over to it and tugged at the door with two hands, his heart struggling under the effort. He was suddenly overcome with a mix of self-pity and loathing.

Inside, it stank of stale fags and urine. He leaned against the cold glass and tussled with his breathing till he'd got the better of it. In the silence, his heart played out an irregular fluttering tune.

He'd already worked out what he was going to say. It would be simple and it would be on his terms. There was something to be said for this dying business. For the first time in his life, he felt he was in charge. Slowly and carefully, he dialled the number and listened to the ringing.

It was a woman who answered. When she asked him which service he required, he told her he wanted to speak to CID. Anyone in particular? she said. She sounded snooty, but he was used to people talking down their noses at him.

'Is Inspector New around?' he asked.

'Inspector New retired a few months back,' she told him.

In that case, he didn't mind, he said. Anybody would do. All he wanted was to get this over with. He wasn't feeling too good, to be honest. Despite the icy cold, he was sweating again, and this twinge in his arm was getting worse. Fortunately, she didn't keep him waiting.

'Hello. DI Jimmy Cotton speaking. Who is this, please?'

'My name's Billy Souter,' he said, 'and I've got some information about the Ruth Dawson case. I know the name of the man who murdered her.'

★   ★   ★

Two weeks later, Christine New was sitting at the dining room table in her dressing gown having breakfast and reading last night's edition of the *Etherley Crier*. She wasn't one for the newspapers as a rule, but it had snowed heavily in the night and the paper boy was obviously using the weather as an excuse not to deliver her *Woman's Realm*. She'd give him a piece of her mind when she next saw him.

Harry wasn't up yet — since his retirement he'd got in the habit of sleeping in. At first it had annoyed her. But now she was starting to see it had some advantages. It meant she could get her chores out of the way while he was in bed. And if she was lucky, there would still be a bit of time to have a second mug of tea and a sit-down when she'd finished. Once he was out of bed, he'd be under feet all day expecting her to wait on him hand and foot.

If only he'd get a hobby. Doreen's husband had an allotment. Jenny's hubby played golf. But her friends' husbands had had regular nine-to-five jobs that had given them a lifetime of evenings and weekends in which to cultivate their pastimes. As a police officer, Harry had worked shifts, sometimes double shifts if it was a big case. He'd had no time for hobbies and no appetite for them either. Perhaps it was too late for him to start pursuing one now.

Her eye was drawn to the headlines. DISCOVERY OF MAN'S BODY IN PHONE BOOTH RESURRECTS INTEREST IN 30-YEAR-OLD UNSOLVED MURDER CASE, she read. Apparently some poor bloke had had a heart attack and died there, she read. He'd only been found in the morning.

10

She shuddered. What a way to die, in the cold and dark all alone and in too much pain to call for help.

'The man has been identified as sixty-year-old Billy Souter,' the report said. 'A police spokesperson said that Souter, who was known to the police, had been in the middle of speaking to a member of CID from the Lancashire Constabulary when the conversation came to an abrupt end. He claimed to have information regarding the murder of seventeen-year-old Ruth Dawson, whose body was discovered under Boldcaster Bridge, Etherley, on February 6th 1958. She'd been strangled.'

Christine remembered this case. The investigation had gone on for months and months. There had been an arrest and a man was charged, if she remembered correctly. But when it went to court, the judge had thrown it out due to lack of evidence, and that had been that. It seemed to go quiet afterward, like the police had given up looking for who'd really done it.

Harry had been a young detective back

then, working such long hours she hardly saw him. She'd just had Angela about a month before, and little Tommy was only two. It had been a bad time for them, her run ragged and with no sleep, him on call all day and night. She sometimes wondered if their marriage had ever recovered after that.

'What are you staring at?'

Harry stood in the doorway. He was dressed, wearing the same shirt he'd had on yesterday. It pulled across his stomach, revealing the white lardy flesh beneath. He used to be so smart, so fit, so handsome once upon a time.

'Oh,' she said. 'You made me jump.'

'Is there a cup of tea in that pot?'

It would be cold now, she told him. He stood there then, like he was waiting for her to come up with a solution. It was obvious the solution he was after was for her to get up and make a fresh pot. Some women had their husbands trained. She'd obviously gone wrong somewhere.

While she bustled about the kitchen — she decided she might as well put some toast on for him to go with his brew

— she called through to him everything she'd just read in the paper. When she got no response, she popped her head round the door.

'Oh,' she said. 'I see you're reading it yourself.'

When he heard her speak, he glanced up from the newspaper and met her gaze. He seemed a million miles away.

'It says this dead man was known to the police,' Christine said.

'Billy Souter,' Harry said. 'He was a grass.'

'You knew him, then?'

Harry nodded. She waited a bit longer, but when it became obvious that this was all she was going to get from him on the subject, she tried another tack. 'After all these years,' she said. 'Do you think they'll reopen the case?'

Harry shrugged and folded the paper up. It was a sign the conversation was over, but she ignored it. 'Maybe they'll want to talk to you.'

'Me? Why?'

She recognised that face. She was starting to irritate him again. Sooner or later she always did. 'On account of you being one of the original team.'

'Is that kettle boiled yet?'

'I'll go and check.'

Back in the kitchen, she went off into one of her little daydreams. She imagined Harry getting a call from the chief inspector. Could he come back? His expertise and experience were needed if they were finally to solve Ruth Dawson's murder after all these years. It'd be good for him, she thought. He'd get his mojo back. More to the point, she would get her house back.

★ ★ ★

The chief constable sat at his desk anticipating the next pearl of wisdom to fall out of Jimmy Cotton's mouth. The young DI stood confidently before him with his daft haircut and wearing that ridiculous suit with the shoulders so wide he looked like he'd smuggled a couple of coat hangers under his jacket. Twenty-three years of age and he thought he knew everything. No doubt that was what a degree from Cambridge University gave you.

Sometimes he wondered what the police force was coming to. Like he'd ever learned anything about policing from books. What was needed to solve a crime, in his opinion, was a sound pair of ears, an excellent pair of eyes, and a nose that could sniff out when someone was telling lies. But apparently this wasn't enough for DI Jimmy Cotton. He wanted files.

There they stood, six deep on the desk in front of him. From the Met and the coroner's office; from the director of prosecutions and from the Crown Court. He was welcome to them.

If Billy Souter had been telling the truth, then it had to be in the public interest to reopen the investigation, Jimmy had insisted after that phone call he'd taken; and it seemed the commissioner had agreed with him. If only Souter could have hung on a bit longer and given the name of that young lass's murderer before he'd dropped down dead, they wouldn't be where they were now. But he'd always been an awkward little so and so, that one. Wherever he was now, he'd be rubbing his dirty hands with glee at all this extra work he was about to cause them.

'I'm very grateful for these, sir,' Jimmy said. 'There's a lot of reading here.'

'Aye, well, you'll enjoy that.'

Jimmy gave a self-deprecating grin. To give him credit, at least he understood when he was having the micky taken.

'I'm not sure I can get through them all on my own, though,' he said.

The chief constable was ready for him. 'You can have WPC Sally Fry,' he said. 'But that's all I can spare.'

'With respect, sir . . . '

The chief constable raised his hand to put an end to any objections he might have. Sally Fry was in her late forties, a woman from round these parts with a sensible head on her shoulders who wouldn't stand for any nonsense. If that young pup went off chasing imaginary rabbits, she'd know how to bring him back to heel.

'Listen, lad. I wasn't involved in this case first time round. I was a serving officer in the army at the time. Germany, among other places. But I do know this much about it. When that poor young lass was murdered, four hundred people were spoken to, ninety-two detectives were involved in the investigation, and a hundred and thirty statements were taken.' He fixed Jimmy with a stern gaze. 'And still her murderer got away with it.'

'Yes, sir.'

'So what makes you think you can come up with the answer now, thirty years later, when memories have faded and some of the key witnesses will have died?'

'I have no idea, sir,' Jimmy said. 'Something may have been overlooked. Somebody may come forward who didn't before. We know allegiances can change. Billy Souter's obviously did.'

Jimmy leaned across the desk and took hold of the files. It was a struggle for him, and it looked like a couple were about to slip through his fingers, but the chief constable had no intention of helping him. He'd asked for the damn things, after all. At the door Jimmy, doing his best to appear unflustered, turned round.

'From what I already know, Ruth Dawson was part of a loving family. Although her father's no longer living, there's an older sister, a younger brother and a mother still alive,' he said. 'Don't we owe it to them to get justice for Ruth?'

The chief constable could stand it no longer. He got to his feet, unable to bear seeing the lad struggle with the door. 'You're right of course,' he said, his hand on the handle. 'You'll not find many as can argue with that.'

Jimmy Cotton threw him a smile of gratitude.

'I hope you get somewhere, son,' the chief constable said, forgetting for a moment that he had a reputation to keep up.

★ ★ ★

Mum hadn't stopped cleaning all week. Luke thought it was like an illness with her. He'd joked about it at first to Miriam over the phone. Just make sure you keep moving when you come round, he'd told her. Otherwise she'll take her feather duster to you.

Inside though he wasn't laughing. He'd seen her like this before. He hadn't been able to cope with it then and he knew he wouldn't be able to cope with it now, even though he was thirty years older. Yes, she'd lost a daughter. But he'd lost a sister *and* a mother, because after Ruth's death, it was as if the woman who'd looked after him for the first twelve years of his life had died too.

Now it was about to start all over again. Strangers pointing at you in the street, muttering to each other behind their hands. Reporters shoving their cameras in your face whenever you stepped outside. Now that the police had dredged things up again, who knew what sort of crackpots would start coming forward giving them all false hopes. It wouldn't have surprised him if the bloke who'd made that call was one such crackpot. People would do anything to get their name in the papers these days.

Where was Miriam? That inspector was due any minute. She'd promised faithfully she'd get here with plenty of time to spare so they could say a prayer with Mum first. Although he wasn't a believer himself — he'd broken his ties with God the day his sister didn't come home — he still kept up a bit of pretence for Mum's sake. Miriam refused to have anything to do with religion, though. Knowing her, she'd decided to be late on purpose.

Luke had tried to tell Mum loads of times that the inspector just wanted to talk to them. That he wasn't interested in whether the nets were mucky or the state of the carpet. But it was like she never even heard him. They all had their own way of coping, he guessed. If his mother's was housework, then his was constantly thinking up ways to prevent this new investigation going ahead. What was to say that this phone call from some old lag wasn't simply a hoax?

There was still time, perhaps, to make a call to the police station to say they'd decided to let sleeping dogs lie. It would be best, surely, for everybody concerned. Mum was up in the bedroom now, getting changed. That would give him five minutes at least to make the call.

But just as he made a move towards the phone, there was a sharp rat-a-tat-tat at the door. It couldn't be Miriam. She still had a key and didn't think twice about using it either, even though he'd reminded her more than once that this wasn't her house anymore. Upstairs, Mum's bedroom door opened and shut. There was an energy in her footsteps. It was almost as if she'd flown downstairs.

'He's here, Luke,' she said. 'Let him in.'

As he passed her, she caught his arm. She looked up at him, her eyes shining. 'This time, Luke,' she said. 'This time we'll get an answer. I feel it in my bones.'

She wanted this. Which meant he had no choice but to open the door to the inspector. What would he be letting in?

1988

Jimmy Cotton had lived in a house like this before he'd escaped to go to university. As soon as he walked in, he was gripped by the same feeling of claustrophobia that attacked him whenever he returned home. There was just too much stuff in here. That three-piece suite was more suited to a stately home than a council house terrace.

There'd been four of them in the room at first, and that had been awkward enough. A battle of the legs and feet had ensued between him and Luke, although it wasn't blows they exchanged but apologies for kicking each other whenever one of them made even the slightest move.

The arrival of the sister five minutes into the meeting further contracted the space. Not to put too fine a point on it, Miriam Bailey was a big woman. Etherley was full of women like her — solid both in physique and character, suspicious and not remotely impressed by a person like himself with letters after his name.

If brother and sister Luke and Miriam were so far keeping their distance, Elsie Dawson was falling over herself to accommodate them. Now that the group was finally complete, she'd disappeared into the kitchen to make tea. He envisaged more awkwardness to follow. With so many opportunities to spill things and drop stuff, what could possibly go right? But to refuse a cup of tea hereabouts was a crime of such epic proportions that his reputation would never recover from it. He was going to have to grin and bear it.

Before they'd left the station this morning, Jimmy had spent a quiet half hour glancing through the newspaper archive file pertaining to the Ruth Dawson case. He'd needed to get a feel for the kind of girl she'd been and how she was thought of by the people who'd known her. Even from the grainy yellowing photographs in that tatty old file, it was obvious she'd been a looker. Perhaps, had she lived, she'd have turned into her older sister. She would, after all, have been forty-six now to Miriam's fifty-three. But frozen in time, she was slender, with even features and natural blonde hair styled in a modest version of the beehive fashion of the time.

Friends described her as clever — she'd managed a total of seven O-Levels at school — and her teachers had encouraged her to stay on into the sixth form. But she'd left at the end of the fifth year and gone to work at McAllister and Smith, which at that time had been the biggest employer in the town. It was still open, though its workforce was sadly diminished, and there were even rumours that the place would close before the year's end. Jimmy had just begun to muse upon the meaning of progress when the rattle of the tea tray distracted him.

'Shall we get on with it, then?' Miriam said, once the tea drinking ceremony had been disposed of, thankfully without incident.

Jimmy caught Sally's eye but she quickly looked away. The twitch of her lips was unmissable, however. He was grateful for her company this morning. She was a woman cut from the same hard-wearing Lancashire cloth as the other two women in the room, and as capable of taking care of herself as Miriam Bailey clearly was. When Sally let it drop that she'd been at school with Luke, she'd heroically exhibited no signs of embarrassment when he made it perfectly clear he had no memory whatsoever of her.

'Well that doesn't surprise me,' Miriam had said. 'He's always been a bit slow on the uptake round girls. That's why he's still living at home with Mum.'

Jimmy hadn't been able to work out if there was cruelty in her jibe, fond sibling teasing, or simply one more example of straight talking northern bluntness similar to her instruction to get a move on. Luke's reaction had been too deadpan for Jimmy to take his cue from him. One of these days he'd have these people worked out. Meanwhile, he had a job to do. Turning to Elsie, who was looking at him expectantly, he asked his question.

'Tell me, Mrs Dawson, about the last time you saw Ruth?'

1958

Elsie stood at the bottom of the stairs. 'Ruth!' she yelled. 'I'll not tell you again. You'll be late for work.'

There was no reply. Elsie sighed. As if she didn't have enough to do in the mornings without having to play nursemaid to a girl who'd be seventeen in less than three months' time. She'd already wasted the best part of twenty minutes trying to locate Luke's football kit for tonight's practice. Any hopes she had of changing the beds before Ernie got back from the night shift were receding fast.

She'd just that second put one foot on the bottom stair when Ruth's door was flung open to reveal her standing there, still in her dressing gown and with a head full of rollers. 'Mam!' she yelled. 'What are you shouting for? It's Thursday, remember?'

Elsie racked her brains. Thursday? What happened Thursdays? She went through the days of the week in her head until finally the penny dropped. Of course — it was Ruth's day for day release. On Thursdays she spent a full day at the Tech, where she learned office skills. She'd been singled out by Mr McAllister after he'd taken one look at her exam results and told her she was wasted in the typing pool. She'd kicked against it at first.

'I like it in the typing pool,' she'd insisted. 'We have a laugh.'

When Ernie had reminded her how she'd been singled out and should therefore be proud of herself, she'd poo-pooed his words. She didn't *want* to be singled out. The other girls would think she was a snob, she'd said. She'd changed her mind in the end, though, once Mr McAllister had pointed out how much more she could make with a few extra qualifications under her belt. Now she was even talking about becoming an accountant.

'I'm off now,' Luke yelled from the kitchen.

He'd gone the back way and shut the door behind him before she could remind him to take his bicycle lamps with him. It'd be dark when he got out of football practice. She ran to the back door, flung it open and called his name, but she got no answer. When she turned round, Ruth was standing in the middle of the kitchen helping herself to a bowl of cereal. Funny, but she managed to look beautiful even with a headful of rollers and spot cream all over her forehead.

'What's to do?' she said, pouring milk over her cornflakes.

'I wanted to catch Luke. He's forgot his bike lights and now I'll be worried to death about him till he's home safe.'

Ruth threw her one of those scornful glances that had always been her speciality. 'Mam! Honest. There's hardly any traffic the way he comes.'

'I know that. But it only takes one car to kill a child.'

Ruth gave a heavy sigh. 'You can be so morbid sometimes, did you know?'

Elsie didn't reply. *Just wait till you're a mother*, she thought. *You'll know exactly what I'm talking about then.*

1988

They were back at the station in the tiny room they'd been allocated, the two of them sitting side by side, the files spread out haphazardly over the desk. Jimmy had asked Sally to go through the one pertaining to the inquest and to make a summary of it for him.

The file was held together by an elastic band and had obviously been well-thumbed. 'Inquest File of Ruth Dawson, May 12–16 1958', it said on the front cover. She was putting off opening it as long as she could. There would be upsetting photographs inside, and she was going to have to psych herself up before she could look at them.

Seeing Luke Dawson this morning after all those years had unsettled her. She'd laughed it off when he said he didn't remember her. Why would he? He was a year above her at school after all, and she'd been just one more insignificant spectacle-wearing underdeveloped teenage girl.

But the fact was she'd had a bit of a thing for him back then. She'd seen him as a tragic figure, wandering the school playgrounds with his sad face, imagining him permanently grieving for his dead sister. One time she'd dared to approach him, to tell him how sorry she was about

Ruth. He'd shrugged awkwardly and muttered something incomprehensible before hoiking his schoolbag onto his shoulder and walking away, head bowed, leaving her feeling like an idiot.

It hadn't lasted, her crush, if it could even have been called a crush. Though she'd often had cause to wonder if she'd ever fully escaped his influence. She didn't think it was a coincidence that soon after the murder of Ruth Dawson, Sally had begun to turn her mind to the idea of joining the police as a career. And now here she was, thirty years later, helping to solve Ruth's murder.

Her mind turned to Elsie Dawson and how composed she been as she'd related the story of the last day she'd spent with Ruth. It must have seemed so inconsequential at the time, that final brief exchange between them. Have a lovely day. You too. Mind how you go, all the usual stuff. And then Ruth, quite out of the blue, had hugged her mother, which had quite taken Elsie aback, she'd told them. Back in those days, English people didn't hug or say I love you every five minutes. That was more the American way. And although Sally had seen people doing it on the telly once or twice, she couldn't really see it catching on in Etherley.

'Don't worry about Luke on his bike,' Ruth had said. 'He won't come to any harm. Neither of us will. We're invincible.'

And that had been that. A kiss, a smile, a wave over the shoulder, and Mrs Dawson never saw her little girl again. Her eyes had shimmered with tears as she repeated their final conversation, and there had been a crack in her voice. Sally didn't have children. She'd been widowed early, so the opportunity had passed her by. Times like these, she couldn't help thinking maybe she'd been lucky in a funny roundabout sort of way. If you didn't have them, you couldn't grieve for them, could you?

Jimmy glanced up from the file he was reading and looked straight at her.

'You'd remember that, wouldn't you?' she said. 'The last words your child ever said to you.'

When Jimmy continued to stare without saying anything back, Sally realised she'd been mistaken. He wasn't looking *at* her. He was looking *through* her. He did that a lot, she was beginning to find out. Sometimes she thought he had a touch of the Sherlock Holmes about him. Did that make her Doctor Watson?

Jimmy was immersed in his thoughts. Back in 1958, Ruth's murder had been headline news. Detectives from the Metropolitan Police had been drafted in to interview hundreds of witnesses. Soldiers with metal detectors had helped search for the murder weapon, which to this day had never been found. Photographic experts were called in to process the hundreds of feet of film shot by police cameramen at the reconstruction. These files contained a mass of information, much of it repeated and some of it contradictory. What it didn't contain was a single shred of forensic evidence whatsoever apart from this one note.

'It says here that Ruth's clothes were returned to her family six months after her murder,' Jimmy said. 'Whose idea was that, do you think?'

Sally looked at Jimmy eagerly. 'I don't know. Is there no clue on the note?'

He shook his head.

'Do you think it's a bit fishy?' she said.

'Fishy? Not particularly. Just amateurish. If those clothes had been stored somewhere safe back then, we could have access to them now. Think of the strides we've made in forensics since 1958. Think of the discoveries that *will* be made in the future.'

'I guess someone probably thought it was the right thing to do once they'd taken fingerprints,' Sally replied.

'You never know; Mrs Dawson may have hung on to them. And if she has, it might not be too late to recover evidence.'

'I'll ring her and ask soon as I've read this.'

It was the motivation she needed to make a start on her task. With trembling fingers, she opened the file. The stark words of the police officer called to the scene struck her not only as poignant, but as if he'd written them in another century not a mere thirty years ago.

'I beg to inform the coroner that Ruth Dawson, age sixteen, of 21, Speakman Road, Etherley, in the county of Lancashire, was found in a collapsed condition at 4.10 on the afternoon of the sixth of February 1958,' Police Constable Robert Jones had written. 'The girl had been strangled.'

*   *   *

'I'm sorry, but my mother isn't home.'

Sally recognised Luke Dawson's voice immediately. It was an attractive one, she thought, managing as it did to retain the short flat vowels of the county while at the same time employing the vocabulary and syntax of someone who'd had an education.

Hadn't Luke gone away to university? What did he do now for a living? she wondered. And why had he chosen to return home to live with his mother? Was it really down to his bashfulness with women, as his sister has teased? Or was it through loyalty to the woman who'd had one daughter taken away by marriage and

34

a second by murder?

'I know it's a long shot,' she said once she'd told him why she was ringing. 'But well, we're pretty short on clues right now.'

'I see. As bad as that, is it?'

He sounded so forlorn that she took a sudden executive decision to fill him in about what she'd discovered earlier in the inquest file. Ruth Dawson was Luke's sister. Didn't he have a right to information? She needed something to help dig her out of the doldrums too. Those dreadful images she'd seen of Ruth post-mortem would remain burned into the retinas of her eyes for a long time. If she could dredge up even a speck of hope from somewhere, it might help both of them feel better.

'I've been going through the witness statements of people in the area at the time,' she said. 'The ambulance drivers, the police, passers-by, your dad.'

'My dad?'

She reminded Luke it was his father who'd identified the body at the morgue.

'Of course,' Luke mumbled. 'I suppose

he must have done.'

Mr Dawson's statement had been brief. He stated simply that he hadn't seen her that day as he'd been working the night shift at his place of employment. He'd been in bed when the police arrived at five o'clock to say that Ruth had had an accident. But he'd added that Ruth had been clever and well-liked and she would be sorely missed. It was at this point that Sally had felt compelled to make an emergency dash to the ladies' toilets. It didn't do to let others catch you in tears in this man's world.

'As you can imagine, the police spoke to hundreds of people and took statements from at least a couple of hundred,' she said.

'So many?'

'What's interesting is that the same three people were mentioned and described by different witnesses. But they've never come forward.'

'Possible suspects?'

'I don't want to get your hopes up, Luke. They could simply be witnesses who stayed silent for perfectly innocent reasons. A man and two young women. My boss is talking to the media with their descriptions. You never know.'

'Thirty years is a long time,' Luke said. 'We were both kids.'

'True enough. Thirty years ago I had pigtails and a brace.'

He smiled. She hadn't seen him smile before. He looked much more approachable when he did. Made her feel less awkward. More sure of herself.

When he asked her if the police planned to re-interview everyone who'd been interviewed previously, she said she didn't know. The chief constable had made a big enough song and dance about sparing her to Jimmy. She could hardly see him coughing up a dozen more officers. Especially as he'd told Jimmy he wasn't convinced that the man who'd made that call from the phone box had been speaking the truth.

'What about the guy who was charged and sent for trial?'

'Justin Hindley? Well, as I'm sure you know, the judge instructed jury to find him not guilty,' Sally said.

'Judges make mistakes though, don't they?' Luke said. 'People spend a lifetime in prison for a crime they didn't commit. By the same reasoning, there's bound to be those who get away with it.'

He had a point. But it wasn't her place to say so.

'I'm sorry,' Luke said. 'I shouldn't be taking out my frustration on you.'

'No need to apologise. I completely understand.'

'Actually I *do* have something to aplogise to you for,' he said after a pause. 'I do remember you from school. It took me a while, but I got there in the end.'

'Well, I wasn't very memorable,' she said, glad he couldn't see her face, which was burning bright red right now.

'You're wrong. You were one of less than half a dozen at school who came up to me and said how sorry you were about Ruth. Most people couldn't even look at me. It was like I had something wrong with me.'

If only she had the courage to confess that she'd had a crush on him once. He was bound to see the funny side. She reminded herself she was in uniform and to stick to her script.

'Luke, I have to go,' she said. 'D'you think you could get your mum to ring me?'

'Better — come round later today when I can guarantee she'll be in.'

'Will you be there too?'

'I'll make sure of it.'

Goodness! Maybe she hadn't lost her touch after all.

★   ★   ★

Justin Hindley gripped the arms of the chair to stop himself shaking. His blood pounded in his ears and his stomach was doing peculiar things. If only he hadn't answered the door. Five minutes ago, he'd been happily making himself lunch, debating whether to have tomato or chutney on his cheese sandwich and looking forward to an afternoon of racing on the telly, mentally spending the imaginary winnings that would be his if his accumulator came up.

When he opened the door and saw him

standing there, it was like he'd landed in a bad dream. He should have stopped him setting foot over the threshold. But all that was in the past now. The judge had instructed the jury to find him not guilty. Policemen had that way with them, though. Leastways, this one did. Like he owned the place. Like he was coming inside whatever you said.

He was gone now. He'd said his piece. But if Justin knew anything about the look in that inspector's eye, he knew this much. He'd be back. He'd been here before. And this time he might not get out of it so easily.

1988

When Sally suggested that Jimmy might like to attend Billy Souter's funeral, he looked at her as if she'd suggested he should come to work tomorrow wearing a dress.

'Why?' he asked her.

'Out of respect,' she replied.

He thought about this for precisely ten

seconds before saying he didn't have time. If those were the sort of manners they taught you at Cambridge University, then she didn't think much of the place, she almost blurted out. But instead she let her face do the talking. She was pretty certain he got the message.

So here she was instead at the entry to the nave, immaculate in uniform, her shoes polished to perfection. There couldn't have been more than a dozen people present, and one of those was the organist, whose performance lent an air of respectful gravity to the proceedings.

As soon as she'd sat down in the second row from the back, she recognised Harry New, who'd retired from the force a couple of months back. He too was sitting on his own across the way from her. When she raised a hand in greeting, to her surprise he beckoned her across. She didn't really want to, but she had no choice really.

In his day, Harry New had had a reputation as the sort of man you wouldn't want to find yourself alone in an empty room with. Reassuringly, he was an old man now; and anyway, if she wasn't safe from his wandering hands in a church with a vicar and a congregation in attendance, where would she be? She scuttled over.

'What are you doing here, Harry?' She spoke quietly so as not to disturb the mood of sombre reflection.

'Same as you, I guess,' he said. 'I knew Souter of old and I wanted to make sure he was definitely dead.'

Among many of her male colleagues, this sort of quip was considered good banter. Up ahead, sitting on the front row was an elderly lady dwarfed by two companions, one on either side. Sally caught a glimpse of a fluttering white hanky as she dabbed her eyes. Souter's mother, she guessed. Sally doubted Harry New's tasteless remark would have raised much of a smile from her.

Steering the subject as far away from the deceased as possible, Sally asked after Harry's wife and how he was finding retirement. He didn't have very much to say about either, so she guessed he was struggling with both. The wife was fine, and he was thinking of getting either a dog or an allotment, he hadn't quite decided which one yet. She quickly picked up that he was far more interested in talking about work than domesticity. He'd read about the reinvestigation into Ruth Dawson's murder, he said. How was it going?

'It's early days,' she said cagily. She'd already got herself in trouble with Jimmy for being too frank with Luke on the phone. When she'd reported their conversation back to him, he'd been far from happy with her. Yes, he knew Luke was family, but it wasn't fair to give him false hopes about possible new suspects, he'd said.

'Of course,' Harry said, interrupting Sally's thoughts. 'My money's still on Justin Hindley.'

'Oh?'

'Suspected him from the moment I clapped eyes on him. I interviewed him myself at least three times, and each time he changed his story.'

Sally made a mental note to check the files so she could compare them herself.

'He had a few learning difficulties, didn't he?' she said. 'Perhaps that accounted for the different variations.'

Harry fixed her with a cynical gaze. It was clear what Harry New thought about learning difficulties.

'Here comes the coffin,' she said with relief as the door of the church opened and the organ music began to swell.

The last funeral she'd been to had been Bob's. Twenty years ago now. They'd not been married five years when he was taken. She still missed him, but only in a vague, fuzzy sort of way. Some days she struggled even to remember his face. When she closed her eyes now, to mutter a silent blessing as the coffin was borne past her, it was Luke Dawson's face she saw, not Bob's.

⋆　⋆　⋆

Someone had recently placed flowers on her grave. It pleased Solace that Ruth's final resting place was so well-tended, unlike many of the graves nearby. People took care of their dead back home in

Lagos, she thought, squatting down low to arrange the flowers she'd brought with her. They were never forgotten.

She picked out the words carved on the headstone. ERNEST ALFRED DAWSON, Beloved Husband and Father, it said, the dates of his birth and death inscribed beneath his name. Then, below, RUTH DAWSON, a beloved sister and daughter cruelly taken from us. 194–1958.

The words were tasteful, Solace thought, and very appropriate too. Once her task was done she had a bit of a struggle to get to her feet. She wasn't as slim as she was, and she'd forgotten how the cold of a British winter could nag at your flesh and bones like a constantly whining dog.

Pulling her scarf more tightly round her neck, she asked herself — and not for the first time — why on earth she'd left her daughter's cosy living room to trek all the way over here in this cold. She didn't even know this man whose coffin would be brought outside any minute now and lowered into the ground.

It was his connection with Ruth

Dawson which she'd read about in the paper that had drawn her to this place. That and something as yet unknown to her. It happened sometimes. Maybe it was a gift. Whatever it was, she would just have to wait for the unknown something to be revealed. On arrival at the church, she'd failed to pluck up enough courage to enter. She was afraid that people would turn and stare at her — a black woman, a stranger, an uninvited guest.

She was happier here in the graveyard, even though the wind felt like an icy slap across her face and she could no longer feel her feet. Because in this place she could talk to Ruth. Tell her how sorry she was for what had happened. And Ruth had answered her; she was sure of it. It was time to speak. All she needed now was for her confessor to appear.

★ ★ ★

She'd sent Luke out, ostensibly to tidy the garden but really to get him out from under her feet. There really was no need for him to take more time off work just to be with her and she'd told him so. In that wry way of his he'd replied that she couldn't get rid of him so easily and that anyway just because he wasn't sitting in his office it didn't mean he wasn't working.

He reminded her he was one of the bosses now. He had his own computer up in the spare bedroom and he could be reached on the phone if they needed him. She knew it was ungrateful of her to want him to go back to work. She was lucky to have a son who felt so close to his mother — there were some mothers who didn't see their sons from one Christmas to another.

But it wasn't right for a man to be so clingy. She sometimes thought that when Ruth had died, Luke had put his own life on hold; and of all of them, he'd suffered most from her death. He'd won himself a place at Oxford, but would he go? No; it was too far to come home at the weekend, he said, and so he'd taken the place at Manchester instead. There was nothing wrong with Manchester University, and he'd got a good a job out of it in the end. But to have a son at Oxford. Well, that would have been something to be even more proud of.

She was using this precious time alone to make one of her Victoria sponges. If that policewoman was coming round again, she didn't want to be offering her a cup of tea without a bit of cake. And it gave her something to do with her hands, the weighing and the mixing and the greasing of the cake tins. Stopped her thinking the same thoughts over and over too, like a spinning record on an automatic record player.

Why did she want to know about that bag of clothes? Did she really think they'd want to keep them? Ruth had been dead six months, and they were still barely getting through each day. But at least they'd made a start at restoring some sort of pattern to their daily lives again.

Luke went to school, came home, did his homework. At weekends he saw his friends. He still played football for the school. Ernie returned to work. Miriam suddenly stopped bringing food and handed responsibility for the housework back to Elsie because she'd just discovered she was pregnant and couldn't cope with two lots of housework.

Miriam's pregnancy was actually a blessing in disguise for Elsie. It meant she had to pull her finger out and start thinking of somebody other than Ruth and her own grief. It meant she was suddenly too busy to dwell on her suspicions too. She'd almost stopped looking at Ernie sideways.

But then that plainclothes officer had walked in with a bundle of clothes he'd said belonged to Ruth. She'd been horrified. Wouldn't even look at them. She'd walked straight out of the room, not even bothered with her coat and bag, and taken herself off to the cemetery; and when she got back she acted as if nothing had happened. Ernie must have realised how she felt, because he didn't bring up the subject of that bundle of clothes ever again.

A few days later, she went down to the bottom of the garden to see how the strawberries were doing, and she noticed the remains of a fire. If there'd been any remnants that refused to burn — buttons, zips, the rubber sole or the tip of a heel — then all she could imagine was that he'd disposed of them by other means. After a while, the blackened grass had grown back green as ever, and there was no sign of what he'd done.

Elsie spooned the mixture into the two tins. It was velvet-soft, and slithered from the bowl into the tins in perfect folds. Something had happened the day Ruth was murdered that she'd failed to tell the police straightaway. And because she'd continued to keep what she knew to herself, it grew increasingly hard to go down to the police station and ask to speak to someone about it. A week turned into a month and a month into a year. Little Rose was born, and Miriam was ill with that infection she'd picked up after the birth, and so she took on the job of looking after of her granddaughter till Miriam was well enough to manage.

Perhaps if Ernie's illness had been more of a lingering one, he'd have opened up to her towards the end. They could have spoken about it. Cleared a few things up. But his death was sudden. Out of the blue. A heart attack. And then he was gone forever. And now she would never know why he'd lied to the police.

★ ★ ★

Unlike Harry New, who'd shot off as soon as the vicar had finished giving the blessing, Sally went with the other members of the congregation to the burial site. Afterwards, she'd offered her condolences to the mother of the deceased on behalf of her colleagues.

Mrs Souter thanked her in a quavering voice. He'd had his troubles, she said, ruining his health with his lifestyle. But he was still her son, and she'd loved him. Then she'd turned to her companions and asked if they could take her back to Highfield now. Sally recognised the name. Highfield Court was an old people's home on the outskirts of Etherley. These two people by her side must have been her carers, then, not her family.

The frail old lady's departure was taken as a sign that there would be no wake for

Billy Souter, and the group began to melt away awkwardly. Sally was making her way cautiously down the crooked icy path and out through the church gate when she heard footsteps behind her and someone calling, 'Officer.'

It was a woman. Large, black, wrapped up against the cold. Sally waited for her to catch up, mildly intrigued as to what she might want. It was a cold day and the stranger's breath came out in short bursts, like smoke from a dragon's jaws. 'I think you must have been sent here for a purpose,' the woman said, offering her hand.

Sally returned the handshake even though her brain was firing warning signals that screamed 'nutter alert'. But ever the true professional, she smiled politely and waited for the woman to speak.

Introducing herself as Solace Farrell, she said she was resident in Lagos, but that she was currently the guest of her daughter and her husband, who'd settled in Etherley.

'You've chosen a bad time of year to visit the UK,' Sally said.

Solace, nodding sagely, agreed. Sadly,

the time of her visit had not been of her own choosing. Her daughter had just given birth to twin girls and she was needed in the nursery.

'So how can I be of assistance?' Sally said once she'd congratulated the new grandmother.

'I think it's more how I can assist you,' Solace Farrell replied.

★   ★   ★

Jimmy was just about ready to throw in the towel. He'd spent most of the morning trying to pin Ruth Dawson's murder on the original suspect, Justin Hindley. He'd been through the file from the Crown Assizes with a fine-toothed comb, then dug out the inquest file again just in case Sally had missed anything. She hadn't.

Once again, he read through the alibis Hindley had provided. They all said he'd arrived home at three in the afternoon and had tea with his mother and two of her two friends. Unless all three respectable church-going women had all been telling lies, of course. But if they had, then there was no way of knowing now, as all three of them were long gone.

He reread the letter Hindley's mother had written to her local MP after the court case too, in which she maintained that her son had been put under the unbearable strain of three interrogations despite the alibis. In the end, he had to agree with her. Poor Justin Hindley had been targeted because he was different.

Sally Fry came bursting into the room, her nose pink and her eyes shining. 'Jimmy, we've had a breakthrough! A new witness has come through! She's called Solace Farrell, and she went to college with Ruth.'

Jimmy closed the file he was reading. A break, at last! He leaned forward, hungry to hear what Sally had discovered. It turned out that Solace Farrell had been sent to the UK to live with her aunt when she was sixteen, and had been given a place at Etherley Technical College to study shorthand and typing full-time with a view to getting a good job and making a new life for herself in England. Of course, she hadn't reckoned on the racism that had been rife at the time, and quickly found herself to be an outcast. The teachers were kind for the most part, but the girls shunned her. Some were openly cruel, refusing to sit with her, dusting a seat with a tissue if she'd previously sat there.

Ruth Dawson had been an exception. She once offered Solace her gloves after spotting her clinging to a radiator because she could no longer bear the cold. When Solace said she couldn't possibly accept them, she'd insisted, saying she had another pair at home. Their friendship might have thrived but for one thing. Ruth only attended college on one day a week, Thursdays.

'And it was on that last Thursday — the last day of Ruth's life — that this happened,' said Sally.

* * *

The cake was out of the oven and had cooled. Elsie had spread it with jam, but Luke had warned her off the cream. The lady police officer might need to write something down, and cream could be a bit messy.

'What would she need to write down?'

She hadn't so much spoken the words as shrieked them. She was a bag of nerves, and Luke could see it. He'd always been good at intuiting her feelings. When he was a little boy, he'd follow her around everywhere, as if he needed to be sure she was okay and he had nothing to worry about.

On that last day — that Thursday — Ernie had come in off the nightshift round about half past ten. The letter had been addressed to both of them. But theirs was a traditional marriage, and official letters were only ever opened by the head of the household.

The letter was from college. It was with regret, the principal wrote, that the college had to inform them that their daughter had been missing classes for the last fortnight. Should it happen one more time, regrettably Ruth's place would be withdrawn and her employer would be notified.

Ernie had gone up in blue smoke. She'd never seen him in such a rage. He'd walked in exhausted and ready for his bed. After he'd read the letter, however, he was suddenly full of energy. She made him have a cup of tea and something to eat, then sent him to bed. If he were to be in the right frame of mind to challenge Ruth about the contents of this letter, then he needed to be able to think clearly.

When he left, she went down to the garden to calm her nerves with a cigarette; smoking had been a secret habit of hers in those days. She was in just as much of a state as Ernest was, but she had to keep calm for Ruth's sake. Ernest wasn't a violent man. But he was a man after all, and men were unpredictable.

When she got back, the bedroom door was open and Ernie's coat and outdoor shoes had gone. She'd read the statement he'd given to the coroner. It had been reprinted in the nationals as well as the locals. In it he'd been very clear. He'd been working the night shift, then come home round about eleven. That much was true. After he'd had something to eat, he went to bed. That was true too. He was in bed all afternoon until the police arrived around five o'clock to tell them Ruth had had an accident. That was a lie.

Luke was staring out of the front window. He looked disappointed. She went over to see what he was looking at. It was the police car. The WPC was standing on the pavement, smoothing her skirt.

'What's he doing here?'

'That's what I was thinking,' Luke said. 'She never said anything about bringing the inspector.'

Elsie felt her legs turn to jelly. Something wasn't right. Last time she'd visited, she remembered thinking how warm Sally came across as being. The kind of girl she'd have liked for her Luke if he could shake himself up enough to even ask a woman out. The inspector too, his manner, his whole bearing, everything about him had revealed him to be a sympathetic man.

But now the two of them looked cold, hard, cut off, like they were here to carry out some difficult and unpleasant business. Had they found out that Ernie had been lying? And that she'd kept his secret all these years?

1958

When Aunty Vi had written to her mother offering to put her up in her house in the small northern town in England where she lived, so she could complete a secretarial course, Solace had leapt at the chance. The north meant *Wuthering Heights* and *Jane Eyre* — romance, mystery, and wild nature. But when she arrived, she was immediately disappointed. England was supposed to be green. But the only colours in Etherley were black, grey and brown. And any hills and moors were hidden by low cloud and smoke from the factory chimneys, or by a foul-tasting smog that squeezed her lungs so tightly she often found herself struggling for breath.

Worse than the smog and the dirt and the drabness was the way people stared.

They gawped at her on the bus; they turned their heads to look at her when she passed them on the street. Hers was the only black face in Etherley, unless you counted Aunty Vi and Uncle Michael.

At first, she'd meet people's gazes with a smile. Rarely was it returned. People simply averted their eyes. So she stopped doing it. Now she kept her eyes fixed on the ground. Only out here, in the park, where the damp and the cold had driven everyone else indoors this lunchtime, did she feel able to lift her gaze. She should have been in the canteen with the other girls, eating the lunch that Aunty had so lovingly prepared for her. But since the day those girls at her table had wrinkled their noses at the homemade curried pasty she'd brought, she'd decided she would never set foot inside that place again. They said her food stank to high heaven and had wafted their hands about as if someone had made a bad smell. One girl stuck her fingers down her throat to mime being sick. The whole thing made Solace feel dirty and disgusting, so now she brought her food outside and ate it walking round the park.

If the weather was too bad even for her to venture outside — and it had to be pretty awful in that case — then she wouldn't eat at all. Going hungry made the afternoons even longer than Solace, who had no friends to distract her, already felt them to be. Towards the end of the day, her head would begin to throb, and she'd start to lose her concentration and make mistakes in her shorthand. Then she'd get into trouble with Miss Salmon, who would humiliate her in front of everyone.

The sound of raised voices caught her attention. Up ahead, past the flowerbeds at the entrance to the children's playground, two people, a girl and a much older man, were arguing. He held her firmly by the wrist while she struggled to get free. Solace dodged behind a tree, afraid of being seen. She knew the girl. It was Ruth, the only person in her class who'd shown any friendliness towards her. It was Ruth who'd lent her the gloves she was wearing now.

From her hiding place, Solace saw

Ruth break away from her captor and stride defiantly away. The man she'd left behind stood and watched her. He called her name two, three times, but she ignored him and kept on walking. He must have got the message because he turned round and walked off the other way, his head and shoulders bowed dejectedly. There were two ways out of the park. The way his exit lay was towards the canal. This way, which was the direction Ruth was heading, led to the back entrance of the college. Her mascara ran down her cheeks in black rivulets.

She called Ruth's name, whereupon Ruth squealed, her eyes wide open in fright as Solace stepped out from her hiding place. She hadn't meant to frighten her. But she couldn't stay where she was much longer. Class would be starting in five minutes.

'I'm sorry,' Solace said. 'I didn't mean to startle you.'

'Well you did!' Ruth said. 'What are you doing hiding behind that tree, anyway?'

Solace didn't want to say. Instead she asked Ruth who the man was.

'My dad,' she said. 'He came all this way to yell at me.' She wiped the back of her hand across her face. Solace scrabbled in her pocket for a handkerchief.

'Here.' She held it out. Ruth shot it a suspicious glance. 'It's clean,' Solace said. 'My aunty sends me out with a clean one every day.'

Ruth gave her a quizzical look, but took the handkerchief anyway and immediately began to scrub her face with it.

'Are you in trouble?' Solace asked.

Ruth sniffed. 'Well, if I am I don't care,' she said. 'He thinks he can tell me what to do. But I'm not a child anymore. I have a boyfriend now. It's my life, not his, and I'll make my own decisions.'

By now, they were at the bottom of the steps leading up to the college. Solace didn't want to pry further, but she had a father of her own and knew all too well how much they enjoyed living your life for you. She wouldn't have dared walk away from him, though. Not unless she wanted

63

a beating when he finally caught up with her.

'I think I just heard the bell,' she said. 'We'd better hurry or we'll get in trouble.'

Ruth tossed her head. 'I'm already in trouble, remember.'

Solace had already reached the top step. She'd have liked to stay talking to Ruth. They could be friends out of this. But she didn't have Ruth's advantages. She was a black girl living on her aunt's charity, and whatever mistakes she might make would count against her twice as much as any Ruth might make.

'I'd better go in,' she said lamely.

'Yeah, you'd better. Have a nice afternoon.'

Ruth's manner hurt her. It was obvious she thought her feeble. Back home she wouldn't have acted this way. She'd have gone running off with Ruth and spent the whole afternoon enjoying herself with her new friend. She still could, if she dared. Run right away from this college and Etherley and England and hop on a plane back home to a place where she belonged.

Ruth had turned her back on Solace now and was walking away. She'd only gone a short distance before she turned round and called out, 'Thanks for the hanky, by the way. I'll make sure I return it.'

Solace watched her till she was just a speck. She hesitated a moment. Funny, people talked about making a decision. But she didn't think it worked like that. What really happened was that decisions made themselves. Right now, she felt as certain as she'd felt about anything ever that this was her last afternoon at Etherley Tech. Tonight she'd tell her aunt and uncle that she was never returning. Then she'd buy a ticket for the next plane home.

1988

'Did you know that your husband went to see Ruth at college on the day she was murdered?'

Elsie stared from one to the other, then back again. It was obvious that today there was to be no tea, no cake and no small talk. Just this interrogation. She hadn't felt so muddled and confused in years. She felt like a small child up before the head teacher for some terrible transgression. Luke's hand nudged her elbow.

'Mum, you don't have to answer this,' he said with a daggers stare at the inspector who'd asked the question.

But it was too late. She'd already opened her mouth and said the words. Yes, she had known. She'd always known. She was tired of keeping it to herself, she told Luke. He needn't try to protect her. She was glad it was finally out in the open.

★ ★ ★

'So what do we do about that, then?'

They were back in the car, negotiating the stream of children who were crossing the road at the end of the school day with the help of the lollipop lady. This time Jimmy was driving. He sensed they were going to be here some time. The lollipop lady was another example of a Lancashire woman of a certain age. This was her patch and he was on it, that much was clear from the way she'd positioned herself squarely in the middle of the road. Only when the last straggler had crossed would she allow them to drive on.

'What *can* we do?' he said. 'He lied. But she can't be held responsible. She didn't make a statement, did she? And it's not as if there's any evidence to prove Ernie Dawson killed his daughter.'

'Elsie swears he was home by two at the latest,' Sally said. 'Time of death was ruled as being between three and three-thirty. So he was in the clear anyway.'

Elsie must have been living with suspicion all these years, Sally thought. Surely her husband must have realised his wife had lost her trust in him? Why hadn't he spoken to her about that visit to the college? You could solve anything by talking about it. So much damage done because they hadn't been honest with each other.

'And you're sure Solace Farrell said

that about Ruth having a boyfriend?'

Jimmy's question jolted Sally out of her ruminations.

'She swore it,' Sally said. 'Remember how she described her wearing a lot of makeup? It sounded like she intended to meet someone, and as if her father arrived just as she was bunking off to meet him.'

Finally, they were moving. Jimmy gave a sarcastic wave to the lollipop lady, who acknowledged it by raising her lollipop — equally sarcastically, he was certain. You just couldn't win with these women. He turned his thoughts back to the case.

Three months after Ruth's murder, the coroner's verdict stated that there was no reason or motive or indeed anything at all to show that she was the intended victim or merely passing. If Solace Farrell had returned to college next day, she'd have heard about Ruth's murder, and her statement would have set the inquiry on a different path entirely. They'd have been looking for a boyfriend.

'Harry New still reckons Justin Hindley for it,' Sally said.

She'd had a quick reread of Hindley's statements, and much as she wished she didn't have to agree with Harry New, he'd been right to say there were a few inconsistencies. Jimmy made that sound he did when he thought the person speaking was talking rubbish; a sort of blowing and puffing through the lips.

'Those interviews would never have been allowed now,' he said. 'He should have had an appropriate adult with him, for one thing. And another, he was interviewed three days on the trot, all at silly times. Twice at seven in the morning and once at midnight when he should have been in bed. No wonder he got muddled.'

Sally decided not to pursue it. She was a mere WPC after all, and Jimmy was the brains. But already she was beginning to hatch a plan.

* * *

Sally found Jimmy in the canteen. He cut a lonely figure sitting on his own in his London suit. She wished she could find him a nice girlfriend; somebody to take him out of himself. He might look a bit happier then. He wasn't a bad-looking lad, with that floppy hair, and he wasn't as averse to deodorant as some of the men she'd had to share a small space with. He appeared to be in some sort of mystic communion with a meat and potato pie. She strolled over and pulled up a chair.

'What's up with that?' she asked.

'Nothing,' he said. 'Just occasionally I'd like a nice salad.'

'For God's sake, don't let anybody hear you say that. Real men don't eat salad hereabouts,' she teased.

He attempted a smile. 'So, what have you been up to?'

'I've been to see Justin Hindley.'

He frowned. 'But why? I thought I said — '

'I know what you said, but it wasn't an order.'

'Not in so many words.'

'Don't you want to know what happened?'

'You're going to tell me anyway.'

'I am,' she said. At this point she took out her notebook, then opened it with a flourish. 'Mr Hindley asked me what I was doing there,' she read, 'because he'd already spoken to the detective yesterday and told him that he'd been telling the truth the first time when he said he didn't strangle Ruth Dawson. And he was telling the truth now too.'

Sally snapped shut her notebook and met Jimmy's puzzled glance with her own smug one. 'You didn't visit him yesterday afternoon, did you?' she said.

'You know I didn't. I was with you at the Dawsons'.'

'Exactly,' she said. 'So who did?'

'I've really no idea. Do you?'

That meat and potato pie was still warm, and the smell it gave off was extremely enticing. 'I do, as a matter of fact,' she said. She gestured to Jimmy's plate. 'You couldn't spare a bit of that, could you? Only, I'm famished.'

He signalled for her to go ahead. Sally reached for his knife and cut it in half. 'Harry New,' she said, picking up the largest half.

It had taken some conniving, but Jimmy had managed to talk his way into the record archives situated deep in the bowels of the magnificent Victorian grey stone building that was Etherley Police Station. The entire department appeared to be under the surveillance of one young woman.

Jimmy would have put her round his age. She had long hair scraped back in a ponytail and wore no make-up. But with those dark eyebrows and the thick black lashes that framed a pair of steady grey eyes, any make-up would have been superfluous. She seemed to be wearing about six jumpers, but perhaps that was because of the temperature. It might have been warmer outside.

'It's because of all the documents,' she told him. 'Things have to be kept cold, otherwise they'll disintegrate.'

With any other girl, he'd have made some stupid wisecrack. Asked her if the same rules applied to her or something. But she didn't look the type to flirt with.

She led him to a large brown box on which was stamped '174A', which he imagined was some sort of code that archivists used.

After a few moments spent shuffling through the box, the girl drew out a buff file and handed it over to him. Jimmy opened it greedily. He was a speed reader, and his memory was almost photographic. Today he was having a little trouble concentrating, though. He could hear the archivist breathing at his shoulder, and that perfume of hers was quite distracting. He told himself to focus. After ten minutes, he had the information he required.

'Thanks for your help,' he said at the door.

'You're welcome,' she said.

He didn't really want to leave right now, even with what he'd just learned running around his brain. 'Interesting job, this,' he said.

She nodded. 'I think so.'

'What qualifications do you need for it?' His brother, who was a builder, would have said there was something wrong with a man who paid more attention to a girl's IQ than to her vital statistics. But Jimmy disagreed.

She suddenly became animated. 'Well, there are lots of different routes,' she said. 'Speaking for myself, I did a history degree.'

'Never,' he said. 'Me too!'

They locked eyes. He'd never believed in love at first sight. Until this moment. 'Look,' he said, 'I'm busy right now. But I'd like to get to know you a bit better. Do you fancy . . . ?'

'Yes,' she said.

★   ★   ★

There was no room for obfuscation when you were standing in front of the chief constable. This wasn't the junior common room at Jimmy's old college. The best thing would be to say what he had to say without further ado. But he didn't know if he had the nerve.

'I'd like you to look at this, sir.'

He held out the file and the chief constable took it. It contained details of

Harry New's career since he'd joined the police in the late forties, right up until his recent retirement.

'Harry New was part of the team investigating Ruth Dawson's murder,' he went on.

'As were a good number of other officers serving at the time,' the chief constable replied.

'Of course.' Jimmy cleared his throat and plodded on. 'He seemed to have a vested interest in getting Justin Hindley put away for it. I think he was desperate to fit him up actually, not to put too fine a point on it.'

'Is that right?'

'I think so. Except he couldn't find any evidence. When WPC Fry went to the funeral of Billy Souter, Harry Fry was there too. There was no reason for his presence other than that he expected a member of the police to be there in the capacity of a mourner. He seemed unusually interested in the progress of the case, WPC Fry said.'

'So which bit of this file do you want me to look at?'

So far, he hadn't been sent packing. This had to be a good sign. 'If you look on the second page, sir, halfway down, you'll see New spent some time with McAllister and Smith, between the end of November 1957 and the end of January 1958. Something to do with advising them on security. Nobody's picked up on that till now. Or if they did, they chose to ignore it.'

The chief was a slow reader. It was painful watching his eyes plod across the page.

'As you know, Ruth Dawson worked with McAllister and Smith,' Jimmy continued. 'I've spoken to Ruth's ex-boss, Tom McAllister. He's an old man now, but he remembers Ruth very well. He had great plans for her, he told me.'

Mr McAllister would be happy to have a chat with him later on that afternoon at his home, he continued. His wife, Linda, would be there too. Linda had been his PA at the time. Over the phone he'd described her as his eyes and ears. Her input would be invaluable, Jimmy added.

Finally, the chief had finished reading.

He raised his eyes. 'What are you actually implying about Harry New, lad?' he said.

Jimmy took a deep breath. 'I think he had something to do with Ruth's murder, sir.' He was suddenly gripped by a strong sense that somehow he had just manufactured his own undoing.

'That's a very serious allegation to make against a fellow officer, Inspector.'

'I understand that, sir,' Jimmy replied. 'Which is why I felt it only proper to inform you that I intend to interview him.'

Another long pause. Then, 'Tell me, Inspector Cotton, what made someone with a degree in history decide to become a police officer?'

Jimmy was used to this sort of derision. He'd hoped the chief would be above it. Seemed like he was wrong. But if he was interested enough to ask, maybe he was interested enough to listen too.

People got the wrong idea about history, he said. They thought it was all about dates and wars and kings and queens. 'But history's all about investigating, sir,' he said. 'One source says one thing, another source says something else. Police work's the same. There are always at least three sides to every story.'

'Well then,' replied the chief as he handed back the file, 'I suppose in that case you'd better get on and start investigating the side that's Harry New's.'

1988

Yesterday, if anyone had told Jimmy that such pretty little villages as Corchester existed barely a twenty-minute drive from Etherley, he wouldn't have believed them. But now he was seeing it with his own eyes. This place had it all: green fields, pretty little grey stone cottages, and best of all, nestled in the valley dip, a whitewashed pub made even more inviting by a backdrop of snow-capped hills. Even the sun had come out this morning. Driving over the stone bridge, it sparkled on the water below, lifting his spirits for the first time in a long while.

He'd like to bring Suranne here, if she'd come, he thought. Maybe take her to that pub for some food and a drink — The Wayfarer, it was called — so they could get to know each other better. Suranne. He'd never heard that name before. It was an old Lancashire name, she'd told him, when he went back to get a copy of Harry New's file. An amalgam of Sarah and Anne. He thought it was the most beautiful name in the world.

He was so busy thinking about her that he took a wrong turn and missed the McAllister house by a good half mile. When he finally reached it, he found it to be an imposing affair hidden by trees, tall and dark, straight from the pages of some gritty Victorian novel about factory workers and their heartless boss.

He was surprised when Mrs McAllister answered the door. She must be a heck of a lot younger than her husband, he decided as he followed her inside. She was wearing jeans and her hair was long and loose. When he introduced himself, she immediately insisted he call her Linda.

'I hope you haven't had a wasted journey,' she said once she'd brought him a rather excellent cup of coffee in a large mug. 'I tried to ring you, but they said you'd already left. Tom's not well at the moment. I'm afraid he's in bed.'

This was a major blow for Jimmy, but he remembered his manners long enough to offer his sympathies and hope it was nothing serious. Her husband suffered with migraines, she replied. The only cure for them was to lie down in a darkened room. But she was sure that she would be able to be of some assistance, she added, since she'd had a position in the office all her working life.

'I'd like to talk to you about a police officer who used to visit the factory once a week or so over a period of two months, roundabout the time of Ruth Dawson's murder,' he said. 'Man by the name of name of Harry New. I don't suppose you remember him, do you?'

Linda's pleasant smile faltered, and her neck and face were suddenly suffused in a rose-pink blush. 'If you're here to talk about Harry New, then it's probably as well my husband's not here,' she said.

'Oh?'

She gave a nervous laugh. 'Harry New used to pursue me round the office whenever he got the chance. Of course, I wasn't married to Tom then. But we were seeing each other. It was meant to be a secret. But in the end, I had to let Harry in on it. I thought it might make him think twice about chasing me.'

'And did it?'

'I think when I gave him the knock-back, he moved on to someone else,' she said with a grin. 'Women were fair game to men like Harry New, Inspector. He had a child and a pregnant wife at the time, or she'd just had a baby, I can't really remember which. He clearly thought her lack of sexual availability gave him carte blanche to try elsewhere.'

Could it have been Ruth he'd moved on to? he wondered. How well had she known Ruth? he asked. Her expression grew serious. Ruth's murder was an awful business, she said. There was rarely a day went by when she didn't think of her. She was the one who'd interviewed Ruth for her first job after leaving school, she said.

And it was she who'd first noticed Ruth's potential and persuaded Tom he should encourage her.

'What was she like?' Jimmy asked.

Linda's face lit up. 'Clever. Sharp. She had a wicked sense of humour. Though she could be cruel, too. Especially about the lads that worked in the factory. She'd pick them up on their grammar and spelling, I remember. And she could be nosy.'

In what way? Jimmy wanted to know.

'It was kind of flattering, I guess,' she said. 'She'd ask me where I bought my clothes and for tips on make-up, stuff like that. She said she liked my style. That I was sophisticated, and she wanted to be sophisticated too, so she could get a more mature boyfriend like I had, because the boys at the factory were morons.'

If only they'd asked her the right questions thirty years ago, Jimmy thought.

'Oh, I didn't tell Ruth about Tom and us, if that's what you're thinking,' she said. 'Like I said, she was sharp. She'd already sussed it.'

'So it seems. How well did Harry New

and Ruth Dawson know each other?'

She thought about it as if for the first time. 'Well enough, I guess. Everybody knew everybody back then. It was like a family.'

'Did Ruth express any interest in him to you at any time? Or was there anything you noticed about he — even the smallest change in her behaviour — that made you think perhaps something had changed in her life?'

Linda furrowed her brow. Jimmy reminded her it was important not to hurry and told her not to discount anything, no matter how small and insignificant or only half-remembered.

She thought for a long time. Finally, she raised her eyes and looked at him. 'As a matter of fact, Inspector,' she said, 'I think there probably was.'

★   ★   ★

It was rare they had visitors to the house. Christine usually met her friends in town, and Harry . . . well, he didn't seem to have any, really. She'd been thrilled to

83

open the door to that nice young detective with the floppy hair. It was just as she'd told Harry last week. The police must want to pick his brains about the Ruth Dawson case.

Harry had been on the sofa flicking through the channels with the remote when she'd led him in. He hadn't seemed very happy when she introduced the visitor. She'd done her best to smooth things over, offering tea, coffee and biscuits, but her hospitality was waved away. The inspector had made it obvious too that he didn't want her in the room. Which was why she was now standing outside it, her ear pressed to the door. She might be falling apart — which was how Harry had described her last night when he'd had one too many whiskies — but there was absolutely nothing wrong with her hearing.

Their conversation had started off exactly as she would have expected it. The inspector wanted to know how long Harry had served with the Lancashire Police and about his involvement with the investigation into Ruth Dawson's murder.

Harry was putting on his charm, she could tell. He did that with strangers. It had been a long time since he'd done it with her.

But then something seemed to change in the inspector's tone. He started asking questions that made it sound like he was interviewing a suspect. Something about, had Harry made a recent visit to the home of a Justin Hindley and threatened him, a suggestion Harry laughed at but otherwise failed to respond to. Then he'd asked him about his connection with the firm of McAllister and Smith. She hadn't been able to hear everything Harry said by way of a reply to this, because his words were muffled by the sound of a passing lorry.

She caught the next question, though. Loud and clear. 'How well did you know Ruth Dawson, Mr New?'

Christine's blood ran cold. Suddenly she was back thirty years. Such a bleak time, it was. Winter, and the boiler on the blink, and all those nappies of Angela's to wash, and little Tommy forever snuffling and sneezing. One night she'd had enough. Harry had told her he had an afternoon off, and she was looking forward to him coming home so he could watch the children while she put her feet up for half an hour. But he didn't turn up till tea time, claiming to have forgotten all about it, demanding his tea. It was clear he'd been drinking. She went ballistic at him crying, weeping, screaming, the lot.

'Have you got another woman, Harry New?' she'd yelled at him.

'No one would ruddy blame me if I had,' he'd said.

She'd marched off to bed then, but not before she'd checked his coat pockets, a habit she'd got into early on in their marriage. If she had found any evidence that he was conducting an affair, she didn't know what she'd do with it. She hadn't got that far. Luckily for her, she'd never actually found anything before. But this time, when she'd slipped her hand inside his overcoat pocket, she pulled out a button.

She'd stood there a long time examining it from every angle, rolling it around in the palm of her hand. It was the button off a duffle coat, cream-coloured, made to look like ivory but probably plastic. What sort of a person wore a duffle coat? she remembered thinking. Not a sophisticated woman, that was for sure. Students wore them, little kids, schoolgirls. She could have put it back where she found it. But instead she carried it upstairs and slipped it inside her jewellery box. At the time, she had no real idea why she'd kept it. But thirty years had intervened. She knew exactly what she was going to do with it now.

★　★　★

They were back in the Dawsons' living room. The atmosphere was strained, thanks no doubt to Jimmy going in rather hard on poor Mrs Dawson last time they were here, thought Sally. Today Elsie was flanked by her son and daughter. Miriam held her mother's hand, occasionally giving it a squeeze to remind her she wasn't alone. Sally's heart went out to the poor woman. She looked as if she hadn't properly slept since their last visit.

Jimmy was bringing the family up to speed with developments. They now knew how he'd become suspicious of New, after Sally had informed him of her visit to Justin Hindley's place. From the description Hindley had given of the man he'd imagined to be a bona fide police inspector, Sally had immediately known it had to be Harry New, pensioned off from the force a couple of months previously. And from there it had been a mere hop, step and jump to a deeper examination of New's file.

Now he was telling them about interviewing New. It had been like getting blood out of a stone, he said. New would admit to nothing, not even that he'd ever so much as passed the time of day with Ruth.

'But that has to be a lie,' Jimmy said, 'because Mrs McAllister said she remembers one occasion when Ruth brought coffee into the office for Mr McAllister and New. She says she noticed Harry eyeing Ruth up.'

Linda had told him that Ruth seemed to enjoy his attention on that occasion, preening and smiling and patting her hair. She also told him what a relief it was for her that Harry New seemed to have transferred his attentions to someone else. After that day, she sensed Ruth was waiting for New, and that Harry was always on the lookout for her too. And she definitely remembered that once, when he'd left his notebook behind, Ruth had pounced on it and gone after him to return it. If only she'd given it more thought at the time, she'd have said it was entirely feasible that the two of them were involved. Except Harry New was a police officer, and you didn't expect the police to be as base as other men, did you? Jimmy hadn't replied to that particular observation.

Jimmy had relayed his conversation with Linda to Sally en route to the Dawsons'. She knew he was worried that when he told the family what he'd learned, they'd think the police had drawn the conclusion that whatever had happened to their daughter, she'd deserved it. She'd flirted, she'd dressed unsuitably, and she'd run after a man.

Somehow he was going to have to find some reassuring words for them.

'Look,' he said, 'Harry New was a married man with a family. A police officer. Ruth was sixteen. She looked like a woman but she was still a child. She didn't know men and she got out of her depth. Remember, she had no reason not to show friendship towards a man she assumed she could trust.'

'That's true,' Sally echoed, addressing her words to Elsie.

Elsie raised her gaze. She needed to say something, she said, to explain why she'd kept quiet all these years about Ernie and his statement.

'Ruth was a clever girl,' she said. 'We were so proud of her when she got all those O-Levels and got picked out for special treatment at the factory. We thought she'd go far. Then we got this letter from the college telling us she'd been getting in late and leaving early. Her marks were down. She was in danger of getting sacked from the factory. We were both so disappointed with her.'

Miriam jumped in. This was the first

time she'd heard about any letter, she said. Luke said the same.

'But really there's no need to explain, Mum,' Miriam said, aware how agitated her mother was becoming. 'You thought she'd end up like me, didn't you? Pregnant and having to get married.'

Elsie was about to object but Miriam stopped her. It was fine, she said. She wasn't accusing them of preferring Ruth to her. She was a mother now herself, and would no doubt do exactly the same thing Dad had done if she caught one of hers messing around.

'It hurts me more than you can imagine to have to admit that for the first time in our lives Ruth had shamed us. But neither of us could admit it to each other,' Elsie said. 'What your kids get up to reflects on you, doesn't it?'

It was a rhetorical question.

'We were guilty of the sin of pride,' she said. 'And where pride's involved, everyone knows what comes next.' Her eyes filled with tears but she blinked them away.

'If you're convinced he did it, then why

haven't you arrested him?' This was the first time Luke had spoken so far.

Sally jumped to Jimmy's defence. 'The only thing we could arrest him for right now is impersonating a police officer,' she said. 'We don't have a shred of evidence that he killed Ruth.'

'All we have is this.' Jimmy dug into his pocket and drew out the button from the duffle coat that Christine New had given him earlier. He explained how he'd got hold of it and the circumstances in which Christine had discovered it. She would be on her way to stay with her sister now, he mused. She needed a few days to think about making some new plans, she'd said. Jimmy got the idea she wouldn't be coming back, whatever the outcome.

At the sight of it, Miriam gave a squeal and jumped up. 'Wait there,' she said. 'Nobody move. I'll be back in five minutes.'

And then she was gone, leaving everyone staring after her, flabbergasted.

★ ★ ★

His confession was written. It was all there. She was an attractive girl and she was giving him the come-on. The day he'd left his notebook behind accidentally on purpose and he heard her footsteps running to catch him up was meant to be the start of it.

They agreed to meet that Thursday lunchtime. He told her they'd go down by the canal where it was quiet. It suited her as much as it suited him. Neither of them could afford to be spotted. She was so late he thought she wasn't going to show up. When she did, her face was all streaked with tears. Her dad had been to college to check up on her, she said.

Billy Souter had been hanging about in the tunnel as they entered, looking for men as usual. That was where they went in those days. As soon as he clocked New, he scurried off, afraid he'd get into trouble. For a grass, it had to be said that he'd kept his secret a long time.

Under the bridge, she let him kiss away her tears. The kisses were exciting, but he wanted more. That was when she began to struggle. He hadn't meant it to end like it did.

* * *

Rob didn't know who first came up with the idea of the service of tribute for Ruth. Tonight the church was packed, lit up by candles. 'We've lived too long in the dark,' Mum had said. 'Now we must have light.' He briefly wondered what kind of funeral Harry New would have had. A lonely one, no doubt. They'd found him dead in his garage at the wheel of his car, his engine running, his confession in a sealed envelope on his lap. Such a miserable end. But Luke wasn't going to lose any sleep over Harry New.

So much had happened in the month since Miriam had shot off without an explanation like that. She'd returned out of breath, carrying a small rusty-looking tin. She wasn't one for sentimentality, Miriam. But she shed a few tears that day. Said she'd always known how much she'd disappointed Mum and Dad when she'd got pregnant so young. For years she'd kept out of their way, especially Dad's.

But with Ruth's death, they'd grown closer. She listened to him when he spoke about Ruth — he couldn't speak about her with Mum, because Mum got too upset. When the police returned Ruth's clothes and he decided to make a bonfire of them, he'd cut off the buttons from her coat and put them away in that tin. He needed something to remember her by, he said.

A few days later, he'd taken the box round to Miriam's for safekeeping, afraid Mum would find them in one of her manic cleaning sessions. The button Inspector Cotton had got from Harry New's wife had matched the ones in the box exactly. Sally had shouted out in surprise. 'Oh, it's just like Cinderella,' she'd said, then blushed to the roots of her hair and started apologising madly.

He'd suspected before that point that she was going to be important in his life. But that moment sealed it. She was here now, sitting next to him, waiting for the service to start. Across the aisle sat the inspector, Jimmy Cotton. Sally had been surprised to see him with a girl, she said. A skinny dark-haired thing with a lot of hair. After the service, they were going to have to make small talk with them. He'd put up with that, for Sally.

Elsie Dawson felt at peace for the first time in years. Finally, Ruth had had justice. As for herself, she felt reconciled — to Miriam, whom she'd always loved but rarely shown affection to, and finally to Ernie. For one brief moment she *had* suspected him, and she was sorry. All he'd ever wanted was the best for his children. When they rebelled, he thought he'd failed, but he hadn't. He was a good man.

She glanced up and caught Luke's eye. He was sitting very close to Sally, she noticed. She was happy for him. All in all, Ruth's legacy was a powerful one. She'd brought them so much closer as a family, and brought Sally into their lives too. She would never forget her lovely, vibrant child. But now, as she rose to the sound of the swelling organ and the first hymn, she felt that what remained of her family finally had her permission to move on.

SOMETHING TO HIDE

Casey spotted Gail from the corner of her eye just as she was counting out her change to pay for her coffee. Remembering she'd been to the coroner's court this morning, and knowing how little she'd been looking forward to it, Casey reckoned her best friend and colleague was going to need cheering up.

'Do you mind if I just pop back and grab a cake?'

The girl at the till glowered at her. 'You'd better be quick,' she said. 'You can see how long the queue is.'

'I'll be one second that's all,' Casey promised, which only encouraged the girl to glower more.

Sadly, the mid-afternoon rush had left the canteen cake display rather depleted. All that remained were a solitary vanilla slice, a sunken blueberry muffin and a rather dry-looking piece of chocolate gateau. *Decisions, decisions,* thought

Casey. No one would have thought, watching her dither like this, that she was a high-ranking DI with the Brockhaven and District Constabulary.

Sensing the mood in the queue about to shift from barely tolerant to borderline mutinous, she decided on the muffin, grabbed it, then squeezed her way back to the till, apologising profusely as she went.

'I'm a pain in the rear end,' she said to the girl at the till. 'But I'm on a mercy mission.' She spoke cheerfully, hoping for a smile at least. But all she got was a look of indifference as the girl stuck out her palm for payment.

Gail looked like she was miles away. Casey guessed she was probably reliving the incident she'd been summoned to report to the court. What a ghastly business it had been. When the landlord of a privately owned flat had discovered the decaying body of one of his tenants and called the police, Gail had been the officer on call. Even to an experienced police sergeant like Gail, a decaying corpse was never something to take in one's stride.

'You look like you need someone or something to take your mind off it.'

Gail jumped slightly at Casey's arrival. 'Oh, hi,' she said. 'That'd be great, actually.'

Casey transferred her coffee and muffin from her tray to the table, propped the tray against the leg of her chair, and sat down. 'So how did it go?' she asked.

'Place was empty,' Gail replied. 'Couldn't have been more than half a dozen of us there.'

'Poor bloke,' Casey murmured.

Gail agreed. 'No friends. No family. Two months he'd been there before he was discovered, Casey.'

'Here. Maybe this'll cheer you up a bit.' Casey slid the muffin across the table.

'I couldn't.'

'Are you kidding? I've risked a lynching getting this for you! And it was the last one.'

'Half then,' Gail conceded. She sliced the muffin in two, keeping the smaller piece for herself. 'Here. Get stuck in,' she said, offering the bigger piece to Casey, who attempted an 'I couldn't possibly' face before falling upon it greedily. She'd never been any good at acting, and besides, she needed some sustenance after the community meeting she'd just been forced to endure.

There was ill feeling locally after a group of protesters had set up camp on a piece of land in nearby Endeby. It had been up to Casey to explain to a meeting of local residents that unless a crime had been committed, the law had no powers to intervene to evict the squatters. It was up the landowner to go to court to obtain an order to move them on, she'd patiently explained, quoting act and paragraph of the law by way of support. Only after he'd done so and the trespassers still refused to move away could the police intervene. It had all got rather rowdy and out of hand, and Casey had been glad to get away.

Personally, she thought the protestors were right to show their disapproval of Giles Seddon, who owned the land. He'd sold it to a conglomerate that wanted to build a number of holiday cottages there. Homes that would only be used for part of the year, when everyone knew the region was desperate for decently priced housing for local people.

'Looks like you've had a morning of it too,' Gail said.

'I've had better,' Casey replied. 'But I'm off tomorrow and the day after, and tonight Dom's treating me to a meal at that new Italian out Hokham Marshes way.'

'Lucky you.'

'I'll let you know what it's like. Perhaps you and Rob could give it a whirl.'

'Chance'd be a fine thing. But we've no babysitter anymore.'

'What happened to the one you had?'

'She went off to university,' Gail replied glumly. 'Great for her. Not so much for us. Now if we want to go out, we have to take Molly with us.'

Molly was lovely. But she was only eight. 'Well, maybe I can help you there,' Casey said. 'I can ask our babysitter, Georgie. Nice girl. Good family. Dad's a GP, mum's a — well, a pillar of the community probably best describes her.'

Gail laughed. 'Makes me feel inadequate.'

'No, honest. She's great. Finlay loves her. No, scratch that. Finlay's *in* love with her.'

Casey had 'discovered' Georgie a couple of years previously after asking her neighbour, Michelle, a teacher at the local secondary school, if she knew of a responsible youngster who fancied a spot of babysitting. Georgie had been in Year 11 at the time, and Michelle, who was head of that particular year group, immediately suggested Georgie. She was in Year 12 now, and as well as the babysitting, she'd acquired a spot of dog walking too, on those days when neither Dom nor Casey were around to walk Treacle, the spaniel whose coat shone like melted chocolate and who'd become as much a part of their family as their eight-year-old son.

'I'll ask her tonight and give you a ring over the weekend,' Casey said.

'Where would I be without you, DI Clunes? You're a true friend.'

'Feeling's mutual, buddy,' Casey replied. 'You not eating that then?' she added, noticing Gail hadn't touched her half of the muffin.

'Oh, go on,' Gail said, pushing her plate across the table. 'I know you only bought it for yourself anyway.'

★   ★   ★

It was midnight on Saturday. Casey, still wearing the dress she'd worn to go out to dinner with Dom, was down on her hands and knees in the living room, examining the coffee stain on her new rug with the same forensic scrupulousness she'd use to examine to a blood stain at a crime scene.

When she and Dom, laughing and joking and relaxed after a night out, pushed open the living room door, they'd been surprised to find Georgie, her angular girlish frame knotted with anxiety, shoes and coat on, her rucksack at her feet, perched on the edge of the settee, ready to leave. Normally she'd linger to chat for a few minutes before either Casey or Dom, depending on whose turn it was to take her home, announced it was time to go. But tonight, she shot out of her seat as soon as she saw them, clearly desperate to be off.

She looked like she'd been crying too, and as soon as Casey saw it, she knew why. There in the middle of her brand-new brightly coloured Mexican rug was a huge brown stain. The rug had cost quite a bit more money than Casey had intended to pay for it because it was a vintage piece, imported from abroad, and the only one of its kind. It had actually cost her double the price she'd admitted to Dom, and even the lower price had shocked him.

'I'm so sorry,' Georgie cried when she saw Casey's shocked expression. 'I don't know how it happened. I'm usually so careful with hot drinks. But my hands were full and Treacle was standing in front of me because he knew I'd got biscuits. I tripped over my bag trying to avoid tripping over him.'

As soon as she finished speaking, she burst into sobs and sank back down into the settee, clutching her head in her hands. Both Casey and Dom did their best to comfort her. It didn't matter; it was just a rug, Dom said. At least she hadn't spilled the coffee all over Treacle, Casey said, a great deal more cheerfully than she felt. When Georgie offered to pay for it, neither of them would hear of it. Accidents happened, and if it hadn't been Georgie who'd spilled something, then it would have been one of them or Finlay or one of his friends, they both insisted.

'So you're not sacking me then?' Georgie said, peering through her dark brown fringe.

Casey put her arm round the poor girl's shoulder for comfort. 'Of course not,' she said. 'Don't be silly.' She remembered her promise to Gail and added that actually, a friend of hers was wondering if she fancied taking on some extra babysitting. 'She has a lovely little girl called Molly, a year or so older than Finlay. She'd be no trouble. And they live quite near you too actually.'

Georgie, her tears dry now, said she'd have to think about it. If it were just up to her, she'd jump at it, she said. But her mum and dad were on at her about her mocks. 'They're always complaining about the late nights. Like I'm some little kid who doesn't know about time management.'

'I'm sure they've only got your interests at heart,' Casey said soothingly. 'This is an important year for you.'

'That's what they keep saying,' Georgie grumbled. 'I just wish they'd trust me to work that out for myself, is all.'

Casey had never heard Georgie speak so disparagingly about her parents before. She'd never met them, but she had spoken to them individually over the phone once or twice when she'd been trying to get through to Georgie. Mr Spencer was a GP and Mrs Spencer was a supporter of good causes and a local magistrate. Casey had seen her photo in the *Brockhaven Gazette* many a time. She was usually holding up one end of a big cheque or shaking the hand of some minor member of the royal family.

Dom glanced at his watch. 'Speaking of time, I'd better run you home, Georgie, or I'll have your mum on the phone to me in the morning.'

After reassuring her yet again that she

wasn't to worry any more about the rug, Georgie left with Dom. Now, alone in the room, with the overhead light shining full on it, Casey realised the stain on the rug was a lot worse than she'd first thought.

You couldn't expect a girl of seventeen to know how best to treat something like that. It wasn't a subject on the curriculum. But if there was a right way and a wrong way, then Georgie had done everything wrong, rubbing it so hard that it stood out like a sore thumb against the rest of the smooth pile. All that rubbing had caused the colours to bleed and run into each other too, as well as spreading the stain even further. Oh, well. What was done was done, she told herself philosophically. Nobody had died.

She switched off the overhead light and turned on the lamp, which automatically made everything look better. She decided to make herself a cup of cocoa and wait for Dom downstairs. Once made, very carefully she carried it back into the living room and placed it gently on the coffee table. There had been enough spills for one night.

She must have fallen asleep, because the next thing she knew, Dom was shaking her and telling her to come to bed. Her cocoa had gone cold and an unappetising skin had formed on top of it.

'Let's just get to bed, Casey,' Dom replied irritably when she asked him what had taken him so long. 'I don't know about you, but I'm bushed.'

What on earth had got into him? Casey wondered, taken aback by such an uncharacteristic display of irritation. She followed him up the stairs, grabbing hold of his hand playfully in a bid to dispel his bad mood.

'You've brought the cold in with you,' she said. 'Your hands are freezing.'

He pulled his hand away and went ahead of her, saying nothing, but disappearing into the bathroom and shutting the door behind him. Casey yawned. He wasn't the only one who was knackered, and tomorrow it was her turn to take Finlay to football. She loved Dom. But when he was tired, he could be the grumpiest person on earth.

★ ★ ★

The next morning, Casey woke up with a hangover. It was made worse by the fact that Dom remained stubbornly asleep no matter how many times she called his name, so that she had to do everything herself. In less than half an hour she'd showered, overseen Finlay's morning toilet, found his football kit, fed both him and the dog, and got the car out of the garage. She could see that when she got back later, she and Dom were going to have to have words. Particularly if the breakfast things were still where she'd left them.

Things didn't improve when she remembered the rug. She felt compelled to stick her head round the living room door before they left, just to punish herself with the sight of it again. It was no use; the rug-cleaning fairy hadn't paid a visit in the night. If anything, in the cold light of day, it looked even worse.

To cap it all, when they eventually arrived at the playing field after a nightmare journey in which she ended up yelling at Finlay for persistently kicking the back of her seat with his football boots and at Treacle for barking crazily at the slightest provocation, it started to rain — a fine drizzle at first that got heavier and heavier as the match went on. Not that it occurred to Mr Brown, the coach, to call a halt to the proceedings. Weather was character-building, apparently.

It was a relief to get back in the car when the match had finished — a game in which Finlay had acquitted himself quite brilliantly, according to Mr Brown. Not that she'd been able to distinguish her son from any of other boys on the field, since by half-time they'd all been covered from head to toe in mud.

'What's that doing in front of our house, Mummy?' said Finlay, his sharp eyes noticing the parked police car the moment Casey turned the corner into their street.

'Don't know, sweetheart,' Casey replied, her heart sinking.

This was meant to be the first of the two days off that were owed to her. But in her job, nothing was ever guaranteed. If there'd been a major crime, then the super would be anxious to pull in as many senior members of the team as possible. They'd probably been trying to contact her by phone, but in her hurry to leave the house, she'd left it behind. Sending an officer to her house to fetch her would have been the logical next step.

As soon as everyone was out of the car and inside again, Casey ordered Finlay to take Treacle into the kitchen to dry him off. She stood outside the living room door for a moment, knowing that sooner or later she was going to have to reveal herself. What would it be? she wondered. Murder, rape, or a simple case of a missing file that only she knew about? She wouldn't be surprised. Any excuse to put an end to her paltry bit of leave.

'Casey!'

Dom took a step towards her. He hadn't shaved, his feet were bare, and it looked as if he'd reached for the first thing he could put his hands on to wear. She recognised Jody Bright immediately, even though she was standing with her back towards her. Slim and straight-backed in her trademark flat shoes and her hair neatly tied back as usual, she turned her head when Dom spoke her name. For someone who usually looked so confident and in control, the young detective looked rather awkward, Casey thought.

Jody was accompanied by a tall burly-looking uniformed officer Casey didn't recognise. She acknowledged him with a polite smile and a nod of the head, which he returned. Jody stepped forward, cleared her throat and spoke.

'It's about Georgie Spencer,' she said. 'I'm afraid she's missing from her parents' home.'

'Her mum's been ringing the house all morning,' Dom butted in. 'I tried to contact you. Only . . . '

'I forgot my phone,' Casey said. She could see it now, on the coffee table. She reached down and picked it up and saw she'd had a number of missed calls and messages, mostly from Dom, but some from a number she vaguely recognised as Georgie's home landline, as well as two or three from the station.

'I don't understand,' she said. 'How can she be missing? Dom took her home last night after she'd been baby-sitting.'

'So she was here then?' Jody said.

'That's her coffee stain on my brand-new rug.'

Jody's gaze flickered over the stain. 'I was wondering about that,' she murmured before returning her gaze to Casey. 'Her mother rang the station at nine o'clock this morning to say her bed hadn't been slept in.'

'That's strange. Presumably you've been round there to talk to her in person?'

'Naturally.' There was a touch of irritation in Jody's voice, as if she suspected Casey, as her superior officer, was criticising her.

'When Mrs Spencer went to wake her up at eight thirty, her bed hadn't been slept in and there was no sign of her anywhere in the house. She tried ringing Georgie several times but her phone went straight to voicemail,' she went on. 'She only rang us once she'd been though all Georgie's friends.'

'Or the ones she knew about at least,' Casey said.

Jody's cheeks reddened. On the defensive again, Casey concluded, even though no criticism had been intended. She'd just been thinking aloud, was all.

'Did you drop her off right outside her house when you took her home?' Casey asked Dom.

'Of course I did,' he said. 'I wasn't going to leave her to walk down that long road on her own at that time of night, was I!' He seemed unnecessarily angry, Casey thought.

'What time did you leave here last night to run her home?' Jody asked him. 'And what time did you get back?'

'Hey! Wait a minute!' Why did she suddenly feel as if her husband were being cross-examined? 'Why exactly are you here, Jody?'

'I'm just doing my job, Casey,' she said.

'Should we be contacting a solicitor?' Casey spoke flippantly. But right now flippant was the last thing she felt.

'Don't be silly Casey,' Jody said. Turning back to Dom, she said, 'I just want to know when you left your house and what time you got back from dropping Georgie off.'

Dom glanced beseechingly at Casey but didn't speak.

'It took us fifteen minutes just now to get here from her house in the rain and the lunchtime traffic. I'm guessing you probably did the round trip in twenty minutes tops at that time of night.'

Still Dom said nothing.

'It was midnight when they left,' Casey said. 'I remember it very clearly.'

'And you remembered what time he got back?'

'Of course!'

But that was a big fat lie. Dom's journey had taken him a great deal longer than twenty minutes. And although she'd tried her damndest to shut it out, she'd been unable to stop that sliver of suspicion from worming its way into her heart.

★ ★ ★

117

'So much for the sisterhood!'

Casey closed the door firmly behind Jody and her silent accomplice. Jody must have loved every minute of this, she called out to Dom. Waltzing into their home sneering at the soft furnishings and doubtless finding fault with what passed for tidiness in the Clunes-Talbot household!

She didn't stop there. 'I should have listened to Gail,' she said. 'She's warned me many a time about DC Bright. She's after your job, Casey; she's told me, more than once.' No doubt it would be all round the office by now where she'd been to this morning. The woman would be in her element, spreading it around that between the two of them she and Dom had managed to lose their babysitter. She could have prattled on indefinitely, big smile plastered to her face, as if she didn't have a care in the world. But beneath the cheerful exterior, her heart was knocking wildly against her ribs with a mix of fear and fury, and she prickled with sweat.

Of course, what she really should do

right now was walk back inside the living room, where Dom still skulked, and have it out with him. Ask him if there was anything he needed to get off his chest. She'd demanded the same thing so many times of suspects that it should come easy.

But how do you ask your husband this question? The man you loved and the father of your child? It was a scenario she just couldn't imagine. Between a man and his wife lay trust. Once that trust was broken, it could never be mended.

'I'm going out.'

All the while she'd been prattling on, she hadn't taken her hand away from the doorknob. While she'd stood there, clutching it, it had been her security blanket. But now it was time to let go of it, open the door, leave the house and take some action.

'You'll need to sort out lunch for you and Finlay,' she said.

She didn't wait for him to ask her where she was going. She wasn't exactly sure herself. But she couldn't remain here, with him, in this house. Right now she didn't think she could bear to be anywhere near him.

★ ★ ★

Casey drove out of Brockhaven inland, past the quaint old tithe cottages where once upon a time the families of the men who worked at the brewery had paid rent, till the brewery decided holiday lets made them more money.

Out along the winding road, she continued before turning left at the golf course. A mile further on, she reached the sign that said Atterlea, the tiny village where Georgie lived with her parents. It was then she knew it wasn't chance that had brought her this way. She just hadn't wanted to admit to herself that Georgie's house had been her destination all along.

She wanted to check that Jody had asked the right questions of the Spencers, and she needed to hear their answers for herself. She wondered if the young DC had jumped the gun, turning up so soon after getting that phone call from

Georgie's parents. Even now, a couple of hours since Jody's visit, technically Georgie couldn't be considered a missing person. Twenty-four hours were meant to pass before anyone could be considered so, unless it was a child. Georgie would be eighteen in four months' time, and she wasn't a vulnerable adolescent. On the contrary, she was spirited, intelligent and keen to get away to university, preferably in London or Manchester or Leeds, where, so she'd confided in Casey, 'stuff happens'. Would Jody have been so keen to follow up her disappearance so promptly, has it not been mentioned that Georgie Spencer had spent the previous evening babysitting little Finlay Talbot?

'Snap out of it Clunes,' she told herself. 'You're getting paranoid.'

It was crazy to think that Jody was out to get her. Like Jody herself had said, she was just doing her job. But thinking outside the obvious box, it was entirely possible that Georgie, once she'd waved goodbye to Dom and let herself inside, had made a phone call to a person or persons unknown to come and pick her up and take her to wherever the party was that night.

How much did they actually know about Georgie? she wondered. How much, in fact, did anyone person ever know about another? By now she'd arrived at the Spencers' modern detached house. The blinds were closed, as if the couple inside were hiding from unwanted visitors. She should have taken the hint, because when Georgie's father finally answered the door after a long wait, he looked grey and drawn, and immediately Casey cursed herself for intruding.

'Who is it, darling? Is it the police?'

Mrs Spencer was at the door now. In the newspaper snaps of Georgie's mum, she'd seen Casey had always found it difficult not to think of her as another middle-class do-gooder, a woman with a smug finger in every pie. But seeing her now, her face waxy with exhaustion and her eyes ringed red with all the tears she must have spilled, she regretted she'd ever thought like that.

There was some confusion at first when Casey tried to explain who she was. Yes, she was the police. But she was also Casey, Finlay's mum.

'The little boy she babysits?' Georgie's father said.

'Can I come in?'

He blinked nervously, then glanced behind him as if he were waiting for his wife's permission to allow her inside.

'You've got a nerve coming round here like this!'

Mrs Spencer, who until now had been hovering behind her husband, pushed him out of the way. She spat out the words.

'I'm sorry.' Casey was taken aback by the venom in her voice. 'I just thought — '

'Our daughter was in your care. And now she's gone!'

'Alex, darling.' Dr Spencer spoke soothingly, but Mrs Spencer was having none of it.

'I think, given the circumstances, it's probably best if you turn round and get right back into your car,' she said, ignoring her husband's entreaties to calm down.

Casey didn't really blame her. 'I'm sorry,' she said.

'Unless you've come here to tell us that our daughter's been found safe and well,' Dr Spencer said, 'then I think it's best if you do as my wife says.'

It was a dejected Casey who made her way slowly back down the drive to her car. She shouldn't have come. Her presence had simply aggravated their grief. They didn't want sympathy. They wanted answers and she had none. Or if she did, then they were answers she personally didn't want to hear.

★   ★   ★

When she let herself into the house, everywhere was quiet apart from the low thrumming of the washing machine. There was no sign of Dom, Finlay or Treacle, and the mess in the kitchen had been tidied away.

Dom didn't use the washing machine as a rule. Not since they'd traded in their ancient model for this new all-singing, all-dancing affair. He claimed it was too complicated; it offered too many choices, and he was afraid of ruining stuff by selecting the wrong program. This morning it looked like he'd overcome his fear.

She stood in front of it, scrutinising the contents of the drum as they went round, straining to make out all the individual items of clothing hiding among the suds. From what she could see, it was all Dom's stuff. She was able to pick out the light grey shirt he'd worn last night, his blue jeans, black socks and black underpants. Round and round they went, a merry dance of arms and legs.

Once she'd seen everything she needed to see, she left the room and stuck her head round the living room door in case Dom was keeping quiet on purpose. There was no sign of him, nor was he the only thing missing. The rug, she noticed, was conspicuous by its absence. What had Dom done with it? she wondered.

There was something distinctly macabre about a missing rug and a washing machine full of clothes worn by a man who'd recently been questioned by the police about his movements the previous night. When her mobile rang, it was a relief; something to take her mind off her gloomy thoughts. Until she realised it was the super and he wasn't ringing her for a friendly chat.

'What the hell are you playing at, Casey?'

She moved the phone away from her ear to stop herself from being deafened.

'I've just had a strongly worded complaint from Mr Spencer over the phone, regarding your earlier visit to their home.'

So his initial question had simply been a rhetorical one, then.

'What did you think you could achieve by going round there and upsetting them like that?'

'It wasn't my intention, sir,' she replied. 'I'm just as concerned about Georgie as they are.'

'You can't have anything to do with this case, Casey,' he went on. 'You're too close to it. Georgie Spencer is your babysitter. She got into your husband's car at midnight. Next morning her room was empty, and according to her mother, she wasn't with any of her friends.'

It was important to keep a level tone even though right now she could feel herself unravelling. She wanted to shout and scream Dom's innocence. Her husband was no killer. The very idea was ludicrous.

She thought of Finlay, who loved his father so much he'd trust him with his life. Dom was honest, straight as a die, physically incapable of hurting a fly. He'd stood by her through thick and thin, defended her against her critics, and would do so again without her even asking him to. 'Diamond Dom' she called him in their private moments. What did it say about her that on such flimsy evidence she was prepared to turn against him?

But in a way she was grateful to the super. To Jody Bright too. It had taken Jody's visit and the super's phone call with all the conjecture and inference they each, albeit in their different ways, sneakily contained, for her own stubborn loyalty to Dom to kick in.

'Is my husband under suspicion, boss?'

Casey said. 'Because if he is, then I think you're barking up the wrong tree. Dom Talbot is not a murderer.'

She hadn't heard the front door open, but when she looked up, Dom was standing in the doorway, gazing at her, his eyes full of gratitude. She offered him only the very weakest of smiles. But it seemed to be enough.

'Thank you,' he mouthed.

She inclined her head ever so slightly in acknowledgement. It was as if a weight had suddenly been lifted from her shoulders. Stupid, stupid suspicion. To come between a man and his wife like this.

'Casey.' The super's stern voice summoned her back to him. 'You're a police officer. You know as well as I do that the way we do our job is by looking at the evidence. What am I supposed to think when the man himself admits to being the last person to see her before she disappears?'

Et tu Brute, Casey thought. She didn't want to talk to the super any longer. She wanted to talk to Dom instead. She was tired of avoiding him. By the look of him, standing there, his gaze fixed on her, it's what he wanted to.

'My battery's on the blink, sir,' she said. 'I'm going to have to say goodbye for now.'

She ended the call and dropped her phone on the settee. Dom took a step towards her.

'Where's Finlay?' she asked him.

'I popped next door. Asked Michelle if she'd have him for a while. She was happy to.'

'And Treacle?'

'She's got him too. They've gone for a walk, the four of them.'

'I'm guessing it must be important then,' Casey said.

Dom nodded. 'I didn't want either of them to see what I have to show you.' He grabbed her hand.

'Where are we going Dom?' a flustered Casey wanted to know.

'I said I need to show you something. It's in the boot of the car.'

★ ★ ★

Casey was in no hurry to announce her arrival. It didn't need much imagination to work out exactly how her colleagues would react as soon as they got wind she was on the premises. Speculation and tittle-tattle — the everyday currency of office life — would have begun already. She was cool with that, if that was what brightened up their day.

What she didn't look forward to so much was the hypocrisy. All those false smiles and welcoming words from people telling her they'd never believed any of that stuff anyway.

'I swear. He stood there, mesmerised by the stain on that rug. It was like he couldn't take his eyes off it. Shifty, that's how I'd describe that look on his face, wouldn't you, Colin?'

DC Jody Bright, of course, lording it over the assembled company. How often had she dined out on this so far today? Casey wondered.

Colin, presumably the silent PC who'd taken up so much room in Casey's living room in his size twelves, mumbled something by way of a reply that she couldn't make out. From the sound of it, Jody had collected quite a little gang around her. There was an awful lot of chatter going on. She wouldn't have been at all surprised if someone was handing round the popcorn and serving fizzy drinks.

'What does he do, her husband?' somebody whose voice she didn't recognise asked.

'Says he's a journalist.' Jody Bright again. 'And a writer. Though *I've* never heard of him.'

'I think *she* earns most of the money.'

She's the cat's mother, Casey was tempted to call out from her hiding place on the other side of the door. She thought she recognised that particular voice. It belonged to some jobsworth who spent his days devising forms for her and others on her pay scale to fill in. She'd always thought there should have been a special place in hell for people like him. She thought it even more so now.

She felt herself growing more and more agitated. Much more of this and she wouldn't be able to control herself. How dare Jody Bright behave in such an unspeakably unprofessional manner? And how dare any of these people hanging round her disrespect her husband like that?

Right now, Dom was sitting in the passenger seat in her car, which she'd parked round the back. As soon as she texted him, he'd be on his way here, and together they'd make their way to the super's office. He wasn't looking forward to the meeting, and neither had she been, much. Until now. Right now the moment couldn't come soon enough.

'Right. I've heard enough of this nonsense.'

Casey had been on the point of bursting in on them. But when she heard Gail speak, she held back. Unlike Gail, however, who was giving her defence of Dom everything she'd got. She'd known him for ages, she said. He was no more a murderer than she was a terrorist. And if Jody thought for one minute that any of her flimsy hypothesising would stick, then she was a worse detective than Gail had ever given her credit for.

Casey decided that this was the perfect moment to make her entrance. It was a delightful picture that greeted her. Jody sat perched on the edge of her desk, red-faced, racking her brains for a comeback. Gail, arms folded over her chest, stood a short distance away, glaring at her. Everyone else seemed to have miraculously melted away. Cowards.

'Have I missed anything?' Casey whipped out her phone and began to text. 'Anyone know if the super's around?' she said, looking up from her phone when she'd finished.

Jody refused to meet her eyes. She suddenly looked very busy and began madly shuffling paper. Gail, on the other hand, was obviously overjoyed to see her friend. Perhaps Casey fancied a coffee? There was a lot to talk about. As far as she knew, the boss was in his office, but he said he didn't want to see anyone.

'He'll see me,' Casey said confidently. 'And he'll see Dom too.' She glanced towards the entrance to the office where Dom, who must have legged it from the car park, hovered. 'Come in, darling,' she said. 'Don't be shy. Everyone's very nice here.'

Then, with her ugliest glare reserved for Jody, she took Dom's hand and led him towards the superintendent's office.

★　★　★

'Are you being serious?' The super looked up from his desk and finally spoke. The expression on his face suggested that he'd seen everything now.

'Dom's car is still in the garage where he parked it last night,' Casey said. 'We thought — no, I insist that forensics bring it in.'

'We came here together. In Casey's,' Dom said.

The super sighed, leaned on his elbows, dug his fists into his cheeks and continued to glare at them in silence. This way he had of treating everyone who stood before him, from the lowliest recruit to the highest-ranking officer, didn't bother Casey. She was used to it. But she could sense Dom's discomfort even without looking at him.

'The super's a good man. He'll understand,' she'd said to him after she'd spent half an hour persuading him that they really had to put an end to this here and now or if they didn't then he *would* be arrested. Not for any crime to do with Georgie Spencer but for wasting police time.

They'd been standing in the garage at the time, both staring into the boot of the car. When Dom, grabbing her by the arm and pulling her outside, said she needed to see what was in there — that it had been an accident, and that when he'd done what he'd done, it had been the worst thing he'd ever had to do in his life and he never wanted to do anything like it again — Casey thought she might just pass out with the shock.

'It's in there,' he said, pointing to an old frayed hessian bag that had once contained something he'd picked up from the garden centre. 'Brace yourself.'

She'd only taken one small peek. But she knew immediately what she'd seen.

'It ran out in front of me and I hit it,' Dom said. 'I'd dropped Georgie off and I was driving home.'

He knew he had no obligation under the law to stop for a cat. But he had to see the damage he'd done. If he could save it, then he would. Dom loved all creatures great and small. He was a big softy where animals were concerned.

'The poor thing,' he said. 'I had to put it out of its misery.'

He'd brought it back so they could bury it. It wore no tag, so they didn't know its name. But he couldn't let it lie there in the open air for the foxes to pick at. He'd told her all this and now he'd shared it with the super, who clearly thought him mad.

Finally the super spoke. 'So when forensics go through your car, the only blood they'll find will be the cat's.'

Dom nodded. 'I've told you the truth,' he said.

'Finally,' Casey muttered.

The super reached for the phone. 'I'm about to commandeer a team to fetch your car in,' he said curtly.

Casey nodded.

'We have to be seen to do things by the

book,' he added. 'But I believe you.'

Dom and Casey exchanged a long look of relief.

'So now we've finished, you can both go home.'

Dom made a move to leave immediately. Casey, however, wasn't so eager to leave the super's office.

'Just one thing though, boss,' she said. 'We still have a missing girl to find. I want you to take DC Jody Bright off the case. And I want you to put me on instead.'

★   ★   ★

Whenever Casey got mad, she cleaned. Dom said she should get mad more often. It was almost lunchtime now. She'd spent the morning blitzing the bedrooms and kitchen, cleaning the bathroom till it sparkled and stripping the beds. The culmination of her housework splurge had been a remarkable feat of multitasking as she'd made her precarious descent downstairs, clinging onto the dirty laundry intended for the washing machine under one arm while wielding the vacuum cleaner with the other.

As she went about her work, she replayed the conversation she'd had with the super yesterday, when she'd dragged Dom into his office to explain himself. Apart from saying that he believed Dom was telling the truth but that as a matter of form they would have to impound his car to check that any blood or fibres they might find in the boot of his car would belong to the dead cat he'd unfortunately hit en route home, and not to Georgie, Casey thought Dom had got off lightly.

Frankly she'd quite enjoyed watching the boss humiliate him in that inimitable way of his she herself had been subjected to so often. But now that Dom had been exonerated, she wanted to be back on the case. Which meant Jody was going to have to come off it.

'Absolutely not,' the super had said.

He'd allocated the case to DC Bright and that was the end of it. She could have pursued it, said something about how unprofessional Jody had been, discussing her suspicions about Dom with the entire office and brought up how much time she'd wasted pursuing Dom when she could have been following other leads. But that would have been personal, and Casey didn't do personal. Instead she did housework. So it looked like she was just going to have to suck it up.

She'd just reached the bottom of the stairs when she heard someone knocking on the back door. Only Michelle, her next-door neighbour, announced herself by coming that way. Casey dropped the vacuum cleaner and hurried to answer it.

'Oh. You're busy. I can come back later if you want,' Michelle said. 'Presuming it *is* you of course,' she added. 'You're hard to make out from behind all that washing!'

She was smartly dressed and in full make-up. Heels too, and a very swish calf-leather briefcase. Casey was more used to seeing the dressed-down version of Michelle, and was reminded just how commanding her neighbour must look to both pupils and the staff at the school where she was deputy principal.

I really ought to make more of an effort with my own presentation, she thought, opening the door wider to let Michelle in. Maybe if she'd changed out of her trackie bottoms and sweatshirt and thought about dragging a comb through her hair before she'd descended on the super in his office yesterday, he might have taken her side against the always neat-as-a-pin Jody Bright.

'Tea? I know I could use one,' she said, grabbing the kettle.

'Tea would be great. If you're sure.'

Casey dumped the sheets in the washer, then put the vacuum cleaner away, switched the kettle on, and poured the washing powder into the dispenser all within the space of about ten seconds.

'Are you all right?' Michelle had been watching all this warily from the middle of the kitchen.

Casey programmed the washing machine before grabbing two mugs, setting them down on the unit and opening the fridge door for the milk. 'What?' she said, pausing briefly. 'Oh. This. Yes, I'm sorry. I need to slow down, I know.'

Michelle put down her briefcase and

took a seat at the kitchen table. 'Have you got it sorted? Whatever it was yesterday with Dom, I mean?' she said.

'What? Oh, that. Yes, we did. You don't take sugar, do you?'

'Just milk please. A dash.'

'Thanks for having Finlay and Treacle, by the way.'

'My pleasure.'

'I saw them outside earlier, before Dom took Finlay off to school,' Michelle said. 'They looked like they were having a prayer meeting.'

'Yes. It's a long story.'

It had been Finlay's suggestion to bury the cat in the back yard under a tree. Although if he hadn't, Casey suspected that sooner or later Dom would have come up with the same idea. They'd done the deed last night. It had taken Dom forever to dig a grave so deep that even Treacle wouldn't have the stamina to unearth the contents. He'd come back inside covered in soil, pouring with sweat and exhausted. Casey suspected it was his penance for his dark deed.

Early this morning, he and Finlay had

held a private ceremony for the cat with no name who happened to be in the wrong place at the wrong time, which was how Dom had described the poor unfortunate creature to their son. Casey had made a feeble excuse as to why she couldn't attend. But the truth was she'd simply gone to bed in a bad mood and woken up in one. And when that happened, it was best if she were left alone.

She felt a great deal better now. In fact, as she handed Michelle her tea and took a sip of her own, she realised her black mood had all but evaporated.

'So. I heard about Georgie,' Michelle said. 'I should be at school now. But I slipped away. Said I was talking to the police.'

'Which technically you are.' Casey took another sip of her tea. 'But I'm not on this case, Michelle,' she added.

'I know. I met the Detective who is. DC Bright?'

'Good. How far has she got?'

Michelle shrugged. 'Why aren't you involved Casey?'

'Another long story. Have you spoken to her yourself?'

Michelle admitted she had, but only briefly. DC Bright was more interested in hearing from Georgie's friends. Which was as it should be, Casey said, though showing so much solidarity with a woman who'd pinned murder on her husband in front of all their colleagues was nearly choking her.

'I did try to speak to her just now,' Michelle said. 'But she didn't seem to want to know me. Actually, she was quite rude. Stuck the palm of her hand in my face to stop me speaking while she answered her phone.'

Jody did that a lot, Casey knew from her own experience.

'So I came here. With this.' She reached for her briefcase and drew out an A4 file. It contained the details of a pupil who'd attended the school the previous year but who'd since moved on, she said. 'I'm probably barking up the wrong tree. But it's at least got to be as useful as getting absolutely nowhere with Georgie's friends. To a girl or boy, all they can come up with is that she told them she was going babysitting on Saturday night and that she couldn't come out Sunday because she had to revise for her mocks.'

While she'd been speaking, Michelle had opened the file and removed three sheets of A4 paper. She passed the first one to Casey. A passport photo attached to the top of the page showed the face of a young boy with dark hair, a scornful mouth and a contemptuous gaze. Underneath were written his name, date of birth and address. Except two addresses had been crossed out and the third one written in such small handwriting that it was hard to decipher what it said.

'Matthew Ferrie,' Michelle said. 'Known as Matt. As you can see, by the time we got to the third address, we'd run out of space.'

'By the look of what's written here, he had a colourful career in the short time he was at the school,' Casey said.

She skimmed through the other two pages of reports. Most of what was written was to do with his behavior, which was generally disruptive; his timekeeping, which was somewhat erratic; and his progress, which appeared to be nonexistent.

'He stayed a term and a half, according to this,' Casey said. 'Left before the final exams, though he seemed to have been predicted good grades.'

'Oh he was a bright one all right. But in the all the time he was with us, he rarely put in a full week.' Michelle tilted her head to one side and glanced wistfully at Matt's photo. 'Such a waste,' she added.

'So what's his connection with Georgie?'

'He and Georgie were friends. He was a year older than her. Well, an academic year, that is. Though he was nearer to two years older, as his birthday was September and hers is August.'

'Georgie's so ambitious,' Casey said, glancing through the reports again. 'It's hard to tell what she'd see in someone whose ambitions didn't match her own.'

Michelle gave Casey a scornful glance. 'Are you kidding? You can see he's a good-looking lad. And have you met her parents? Pushy is not the word. Of course she's going to fall for a bad boy like Matt. His own parents are itinerant workers. They go where the money is. Stay a while then move on, taking Matthew with them.'

'She never mentioned a boyfriend to me,' Casey said.

'Well, she wouldn't, would she? In case you accidentally mentioned it to Mum and Dad.'

'I suppose not.'

'But it was obvious there was something going on. They were like magnets. On days he didn't show up, Georgie would be downcast. But when he was there, well, she was a different person. 'Joyous' is how I'd describe her.'

Casey mulled over what she'd learned. Matthew Ferrie had left the school a week before the official end of the summer term. Presumably his family had left Brockhaven and gone somewhere where there was more profit to be had. It was October now. The summer season was long over. The family could be anywhere. Abroad, even.

'Do you think they could have run away together?'

Michelle voiced the exact same suspicion Casey had begun to harbour. 'It's not unfeasible,' she replied.

Something stirred in Casey's memory. The last time she'd seen Georgie, she'd seemed jumpy. Was that just to do with her anxiety about spilling coffee on Casey's precious rug? Or had her jumpiness actually precipitated her accident? And then there was the way she'd spoken about her parents.

She'd never thought of Georgie as a troubled teen before. But for five minutes, when she complained about her parents' overprotectiveness towards her, Casey had been reminded of the girls she ran into in her working life: the runaways, the lost souls, the young women who'd been harmed so much by society that their only way of getting their own back was to be as troublesome as they could be. There was another thing bugging her too. It picked at a corner of her memory. But right now it stubbornly refused to reveal itself.

'I honestly have no idea what's happened to Georgie,' Casey replied. 'But I'm going to do my best to find out.'

Even if it meant ignoring the super's orders and elbowing Jody Bright out of the way, she decided as she waved goodbye to Michelle. Funny how all that housework had cleared her head and stiffened her resolve. As she closed the door behind her, she heard the house phone ring. It was the super. She thought he must have been ringing to confirm arrangements for impounding Dom's phone. But she was wrong.

'Your man's in the clear,' he said gruffly, not bothering with the hello and how are you bit. 'A couple of the neighbours saw Georgie Spencer get out of Dom's car, run up the drive and let herself inside, then close the door behind her.'

'And they definitely saw him drive off alone?' she said.

'Yes.'

'So you won't be impounding his car?'

'No. Not with these witness statements. If there were the slightest doubt, then we'd go for it. But the two people came forward independently. And they didn't know each other. They just both happened to be closing their bedroom curtains at the same time.'

'Did they see anything else? Like her coming back out of the house, for instance?'

There was a long pause at the other end.

'You're not on this job, Casey. I thought we'd already settled this point.'

'Georgie's my babysitter. She's a friend of the family.'

'Precisely. I rest my case.'

She'd never met so stubborn a man in her entire life. Finlay had nothing on him. 'So what now?' she asked him.

'So nothing. I guess you come back on shift after your leave, as usual.'

'Right,' she replied curtly. 'I'll see you tomorrow, then.'

She ought to let Dom know he was definitely in the clear. But if she spoke to him now, she didn't think she'd be able to hold back how she felt about the super's intransigence.

She strode into the living room, wondering what to do instead. It was looking particularly grim in here. The other day she thought she'd spotted a clutch of pine needles from the Christmas tree lurking behind the TV. Doubtless she'd find a few sweet wrappers jammed between the seat cushions too if she rummaged hard enough. It was only a couple of months till next Christmas. She really ought to sort it out till the festive jamboree began again.

In fact, this settled it. Only another bout of housework was going to rid her of her pent-up rage. She'd been right about the sweet wrappers, she mused, tipping the settee cushions onto the floor. But there was something else there too.

A bit of paper, screwed up. She reached for it and smoothed it out. On it was written a telephone number in faint blue ink. It wasn't her writing, and anyway she'd have remembered if she'd written it. Nor was it Dom's, who used the fancy continental seven with a line through it. It wasn't the writing of a child either. And although Treacle had many talents, holding a pen was not one of them.

She held the piece of paper between her fingers and stared at the number for a long time. All at once a something clicked in her head. On Saturday night, when they'd left, Georgie had been sitting in this exact spot on the settee if she remembered right. Her bag had been at her feet. But it hadn't been her usual bag, which was blue with bright red lollipops all over it.

This bag had been much bigger. A rucksack, in fact. The kind of bag you might pack if you intended going off somewhere for a few days, a week, or even longer. The more she thought about it the more obvious it seemed to her. Georgie had planned her escape and she didn't want to be found.

But whose was this number? There was only one way to find out. It rang for a long time before switching to voicemail. The speaker was female, with a perky voice and an accent Casey would have described as coming somewhere south of Brockhaven but west of Birmingham. The speaker asked her to leave a message. She didn't of course. Instead she rang Linda in the office.

'Find out who this number belongs to, will you?' she said. 'And ring me right back when you do.'

* * *

As soon as Casey got her answer, she set out for work. Pity about the living room. It was just going to have to stay a mess until the next time she needed to take out her frustrations. But this was more important.

The first person her gaze landed on as she walked in was Gail. To say she looked harassed was an understatement. From the way she was holding the receiver so far away from her ear, she guessed the person on the other end was yelling at her.

'Yes. I do indeed see. And I appreciate you quoting Section 61 of the Criminal Justice and Public Order Act 1994 at me,' she said.

Gail glanced up, caught Casey's eye and gritted her teeth. Casey made a 'fancy a coffee sign' to which Gail clasped her throat as if to say she were dying for one.

'I do see that the situation has changed since you last got in touch with us, and — '

Another interruption. It had to be a man on the other end of the line, Casey decided. Men never let a woman finish what she was saying, in her experience.

'I promise we'll send an officer round to assess the situation before it gets dark,' Gail said. 'No, I can't say exactly when. But it *will* happen.'

She glanced up again, rolled her eyes and crossed her fingers. 'Giles Seddon,' she mouthed.

What could he want? Casey wondered. Trouble on his land again, by the sound of it.

'You're not due back till tomorrow,' Gail said, finally off the phone and away from her desk.

'I need to speak to Jody,' Casey said. 'I have to tell her what I know about Georgie.'

Gail's gaze slid away from Casey to the

153

door of the super's office; and Casey, following it, saw a rather dismayed-looking Jody emerge. She looked even more dismayed when she saw Casey standing there.

'Oh,' she said. 'You're back. The super will be glad. He said if I saw you to tell him he wants a word.'

She slid past, lips tight, eyes on the ground. Casey and Gail exchanged a glance.

'Looks like we're going to have to postpone the coffee,' Gail said.

'He probably wants to remind me exactly who's in charge,' Casey said. 'Oh well, here goes.'

She marched across the room to his door and rapped confidently on it to prove just how little he scared her.

'Who is it?'

Casey pushed open the door.

'I believe you wanted to see me,' she said.

The super looked up from his desk. His expression didn't alter when he saw who it was. The word 'inscrutable' had been invented just for him, Casey was convinced.

'Come in and close the door.'

Casey stood by his desk. She wouldn't sit till he invited her to.

'You asked me a question when I rang you earlier,' he said.

'Did I, sir?'

'You wondered if the two individuals who'd seen Georgie Spencer let herself into her house saw her come out again.'

'That's right. And you couldn't tell me the answer.'

'That's because no one ever asked them the question.'

Ah, so that was the reason for Jody looking like she'd just been put in detention by the headmaster just now.

'Tell me what *you* think this case is all about, Casey,' he said.

She kept it brief. That was how the super liked things. She told him about her conversation with her neighbour and everything she'd learned about Matthew Ferrie's connection with Georgie.

She told him about the rucksack and how it differed from the bag Georgie usually brought when she came to babysit. And then she told him about the scrap of paper with the phone number on it that she'd discovered shoved down the side of her settee and how when she'd tried to ring it, it had gone straight to voicemail so she'd immediately rung up Linda, who got back to her half an hour later to tell her the phone was an unregistered pay-as-you go phone so it couldn't be traced.

'You did all this on your morning off?' the super said.

She nodded. 'I didn't seek Michelle out. She came to me. She tried to speak to Jody, only she was busy.'

The super folded his arms and fixed Casey with a lugubrious stare. 'You've told me more in two minutes than DC Bright has told me in two days,' he said. 'You're back on the case, DI Clunes. That'll be all.'

★　★　★

Casey had felt nervous about making a return visit to the Spencer family home. In fact, she'd almost chickened out and sent someone else in her place. But then

156

she'd had a stern word with her reflection in the mirror in the ladies' loos. So now here she was, sitting in the Spencers' living room cluttered with half-empty mugs of cold coffee and trying to ignore the tension between them while she explained that she'd taken over the case.

'I realise you may feel uncomfortable about the change,' Casey said. 'But my super thought that in the long run it would be more appropriate if a more senior officer was in charge.'

'More appropriate' hadn't actually been the phrase he'd used. When the super got angry, he had a tendency to substitute his usual vocabulary for language so colourful it would make a pub landlord blush. This was what had happened when he learned that Jody hadn't yet got round to asking the Spencers for an up-to-date photo of their missing daughter for circulation in the media. Casey was here now to ask for the photo it had slipped Jody's mind to demand.

Only a couple of days had passed since her last visit, but the change in the appearance of Georgie's parents was quite shocking. Mrs Spencer seemed to have chosen her ill-assorted outfit with her eyes closed, and Dr Spencer looked even worse — haggard, drawn, his complexion almost grey. He'd barely met Casey's gaze in all the time she'd been here. It was this seeming lack of interest in what she was saying, as if he had something else far more important on his mind, that made Casey feel more comfortable with addressing all her remarks to Mrs Spencer.

The longer she sat there, the more obvious it became that the couple were barely on speaking terms. Given what had happened on her previous visit, she'd anticipated *some* hostility. But she'd expected it to be directed to herself, not at each other. She reminded herself there was no one way to experience grief. It drew some couples together and drove others apart. How would she and Dom react in similar circumstances? she wondered. Pray God they'd never have to find out.

'Actually, I'm glad you've come,' Mrs

Spencer said. 'It gives me the chance to apologise for my behaviour last time.'

'It's perfectly understandable, Mrs Spencer,' Casey said.

'No. It's not. I was mad to think your husband was connected with Georgie's disappearance in any way. I can't think what came over me.'

Dr Spencer spoke for the first time. 'OK, you've made your point, Alex,' he said. 'I'm sure Inspector Clunes wants to get on. Shouldn't you be looking for that photo of Georgie? That's what she's here for, after all.'

Mrs Spencer turned pink at her husband's reprimand. She looked as if she were about to say something equally harsh in return but must have thought better of it.

'Yes. Of course,' she said instead.

She took her time getting up, smoothing her skirt repeatedly before wandering over to the door.

'Everything's on the computer nowadays, isn't it?' she said from the doorway. 'I can't remember when I last held a real photograph of Georgie, you know; a proper one in a frame.' Her eyes began to mist over. 'All those school photos. Every year they have them done, don't they?' Her voice began to break. 'I still have them in a drawer somewhere. I can't bear to . . . '

One heart-wrenching sob cut off the rest of her words. She stood there looking lost, struggling to regain control.

'Oh, for God's sake. *I'll* do it.'

Dr Spencer leapt out of his chair and stomped across the room like a stroppy teenager, catching his wife's shoulder as he pushed his way past her. Casey had rarely felt more like an intruder in her life.

'You must excuse my husband, DI Clunes,' Mrs Spencer said when he'd gone. 'He's not quite himself.'

'No, I can see that.'

So far, Casey hadn't mentioned Matt Ferrie. Perhaps now, with Dr Spencer out of the way, would be the right time. Mothers tended to react in a more measured way when it came to young men leading their daughters astray.

'Did Georgie ever mention a boy called

160

Matthew Ferrie, Mrs Spencer?' she said.

Mrs Spencer, back in her chair again, looked at Casey with a bewildered expression.

'Boy? What boy? My daughter had no time for boys, Inspector. She was studying for her A-Levels. *Is* studying for her A-Levels, I mean, of course.'

'Of course.'

She wondered if she'd be just as blind to what was really going on in Finlay's life when he reached Georgie's age as Alex Spencer appeared to be. She explained exactly who Matthew was and what his relationship with Georgie had been.

'And this was common knowledge among Georgie's friends, was it? Why did none of them mention him to me? I rang every single one and no one said anything about a Matthew Ferrie.'

Well, that was hardly surprising. If Georgie hung out with girls like herself from respectable middle-class families, then it would be a brave friend who would dare bring up Matt's name in front of Georgie's mother. She told Mrs Spencer there was a possibility she might have met up with Matthew after Dom had dropped her off at home.

'She was carrying a rucksack the night she came to our house,' she said. 'Not her usual bag. You know, the blue one with the red lollipops stamped all over it.'

'That's right. I remember now. We were getting ready to go out. She'd left it in the hall and I tripped up over it.' Her mouth began to tremble. 'I told her off. Shouted at her for leaving it where someone could trip over it. The last words I spoke to her were harsh ones. May God forgive me.'

'Don't upset yourself again, please, Mrs Spencer. Georgie will come back and then you'll be able to tell her off all over again.'

'You really think so?'

'Yes.'

'She told me the handle on her blue bag was broken. And that was why she was using her rucksack. Funny, but I've only just remembered.'

'That bag,' Casey said. 'I suppose she threw it out?'

'I don't know. The officers who came took her room apart looking for clues.

They wanted me to go in with them to help. But I couldn't. I sent Adrian instead.'

She glanced up the stairs and there he was, coming down, a copy of a photo of Georgie in his hand.

'Here,' he said when he reached the bottom of the stairs.

Casey took it from him. It was a lovely picture. Whoever had taken it had caught Georgie off guard, at her most natural. She was sitting at her computer, and someone must have come into her room or called her name, because in the picture she was looking up, caught unawares by the photographer.

'I took that,' Dr Spencer said.

'It's lovely,' Casey said.

The two of them stood there admiring it in silence for a long time. Then Mrs Spencer spoke. 'Did you see Georgie's blue school bag in her room when you went in with the police?'

'Who wants to know?' Dr Spencer said gruffly.

'The inspector thinks it might be significant.'

'Maybe we can take a look together, Dr Spencer.' Casey put a gentle hand on his arm.

He considered her question for a moment. 'Okay,' he said at last. 'Follow me.'

Upstairs in Georgie's room, Dr Spencer found the bag immediately, shoved right at the back of the wardrobe. 'Is this it?'

Casey thanked him and took it from him.

'Why is it so important?' he asked.

She inspected the bag from every angle. So much for a broken handle. The bag was as good as new. In a way, discovering this gave Casey hope. It must surely have meant that Georgie had lied about it being broken for a reason, and the reason had to be because she'd planned her own disappearance. Wherever she was now, she was there of her own free will with a person she'd arranged to be with. Was this person Matthew Ferrie? It was looking more and more likely.

Casey still had those addresses Michelle had given her. Maybe the Ferries had left a forwarding address or some hint at least about where they might have been heading when they'd left Brockhaven three months ago. She immediately decided that their last known address would be her next port of call.

She was going to have to hand over that photograph of Matt too, to the media. Two young good-looking people like Georgie wouldn't stay unrecognised for long, once their images hit the papers.

★ ★ ★

41 Dove Road was situated on the New Estate out on the Endeby Road. Time had done its worst to the once spanking-new council estate. Only a few of the houses remained in the hands of Brockhaven Council now. Some had been bought by their original occupiers back in the eighties, and like the neighbouring council houses were well-maintained.

By far the majority, however, had been sold on to private landlords and weren't in such good nick. The address she had for the Ferries' last known residence was

165

one such property. It was in sore need of renovation, and the front garden had clearly been a stranger to a lawnmower for a long time.

Observing the tangle of weeds as she made her way up the path to the front door, Casey was reminded that her own garden was in great need of some TLC. The lawnmower had died a few weeks previously, and she'd been meaning to replace it so she, or rather Dom, could give the lawn one final mow before the dark days of winter set in. A couple of miles up the road, just past Endeby and out the other side, was the big garden centre. Maybe it would be a good idea to swing by and see if she could find a replacement. It wouldn't be too far out of her way, and it would be an opportunity to see what was happening at the protest camp too. She'd heard all about Giles Seddon's irate call from Gail yesterday when the two of them had finally managed to find time to grab a coffee. According to Gail, more and more people were turning up to join the hardcore original protestors, who were strongly objecting to Seddon's plans to build a clutch of holiday cottages on the site.

The trouble — or the trouble for Giles Seddon, at least — was that most of the people who came to protest left at the end of every day, causing no real trouble and leaving only the resolute hard core to endure the increasingly chilly nights in their camper vans. No matter how many times Seddon had been told that unless the protestors broke the law in some way, then the police couldn't just march in and evict the protestors, he continued to harangue the station day and night, demanding that they not only be thrown off his land but slung into the cells too.

According to Gail, he had a bee in his bonnet about one particular protestor, a man who went by the name of Dengo Hartley, whom he singled out as the spokesman for the group. The individual in question appeared to have an excellent ability to get right under Seddon's skin, apparently. 'Arrogant and rude' was how Seddon had described him, to which Casey had remarked that he and Seddon sounded like soulmates. She'd also joked that perhaps the best person to go over there and bang their heads together would be Jody Bright, since when it came to arrogance and rudeness, there weren't many who could beat her. She'd left Gail mulling over the idea.

From inside number 41 came the noise of a dog barking, then a woman's voice loudly challenging it to be quiet as her footsteps clattered down the stairs. There was the sound of the bolt being drawn back before finally the door opened to reveal a woman in her fifties, her head full of rollers. One hand held on for dear life to the collar of the excited dog as it strained to break free while the other drew her skimpy dressing gown closer.

The woman stared at her suspiciously, swore at the dog, then asked Casey what she wanted. When Casey introduced herself and explained that she was looking for a family named Ferrie, the woman immediately apologised for her language.

'Think nothing of it of it,' Casey said. 'I swear at our dog all the time.'

'These Ferries though,' the woman said. 'They moved out months ago.'

'I just wondered if they'd left a forwarding address.'

'No. They left a rotten mess behind though,' the woman replied. 'Took me a week to make the place habitable.'

The dog, desperate to have a sniff of Casey, was barking even louder now. The woman swore some more.

'It's the son I need to locate.' Casey fished Matthew's photo from her folder and handed it over to the woman, rescuing it from the jaws of the dog along with her own hand in the nick of time.

'Oh, so that's Matthew Ferrie,' the woman said.

So she recognised him! Casey's hopes were up now.

'Try number 46 opposite. They have a daughter. When I first arrived, I'd see them — this lad and the girl — from my window doing their courting, sitting on the wall.'

'Courting'. Now there was a word Casey hadn't heard in a long while. She thanked the woman and crossed the road.

Finally she was getting somewhere. Number 46 wasn't any more salubrious than the last house, but at least she was spared a barking dog. This time the door was opened immediately. It seemed the woman who answered had apparently been expecting someone.

'You're early. We wasn't expecting you till three.' She turned her head and called out to someone behind her. 'Chloe,' she said, 'the midwife's here.' Turning back to Casey, she said she'd better come in.

'I think there's been some mistake,' Casey said.

She explained who she was and what she wanted. The woman's expression darkened at the mention of Matthew Ferrie's name. Casey caught a sudden glimpse of someone else hovering behind the woman. A young girl, pale and sad-eyed. And very pregnant.

'No,' the woman said at last, 'I haven't got a forwarding address. He made very sure of that when he left my Chloe in this condition.'

★ ★ ★

Casey was so caught up in her tangled thoughts that she completely missed the opportunity to have a closer look at the protest site on Giles Seddon's field. She spotted a cluster of people, two or three camper vans, and the merest glimpse of a banner flapping in the breeze. But the only words she had time to read were 'HANDS OFF'. In her rear-view mirror, she thought she saw a car she recognised as Jody Bright's parked at the side of the road. Either she was inside hiding from the protestors, or she was out on the field, right in the thick of it.

Well, thankfully this protest was none of her own business. She had other things to think about. Did Matthew Ferrie know he was about to become a father? More importantly, did Georgie Spencer? Would she really have run off with him if she'd known he'd not only been two-timing her but that he'd got another girl pregnant? That didn't sound like the Georgie she knew.

It was only when she'd driven on for another three miles that she realised that not only had she missed her chance to get a closer look at the protest site, but she'd totally forgotten about stopping at the garden centre too. Well, at least Dom would be happy when he learned he'd won another reprieve from mowing the lawn.

★ ★ ★

Casey couldn't settle to anything. For the last half hour she'd been on and off her mobile, checking Brockhaven Police's Twitter feed to see if Georgie and Matthew's images had been posted. She wanted it to be tomorrow, when she could be sure that the images had gone out to the newspapers and were being circulated on the Internet too. Hopefully when that happened, sightings would begin.

'What's the matter?' Dom, his sleeves rolled up, came back from the bathroom, where he'd been running Finlay's bath. 'You're not still on that mobile?'

'Sorry.' She only raised her eyes for a moment to speak to him, but when she lowered them again she saw that finally the photos were up, alongside details of

172

how to contact the police should any member of the public spot either Georgie or Matt. 'I need to speak to Finlay,' she said, and headed for the door. She'd suddenly had an idea.

'Well make sure you knock first,' Dom said. 'He's suddenly getting very shy about being naked.'

But Finlay was already out of the bathroom by the time she reached the landing. *That must have been the quickest bath in history*, she thought as she picked up the towel he'd left on the floor and replaced it on the radiator. She stood at the door of his bedroom and watched him doing up the buttons on his pyjama top, head down, the tip of his tongue sticking out while he concentrated to get each button in the correct hole.

'Hi, there,' she said.

Finlay turned at the sound of Casey's hello and grinned. His hair was still damp and his face was shiny from the bath. He asked her if she'd read him a chapter of his book. Even though he could read perfectly well on his own these days, he still enjoyed her reading to him from time to time, and Casey was always happy to do it. There were some days when she caught no more than a glimpse of her son because of the demands of her job. When the opportunity arose to spend quality time with him, then she'd snatch it with both hands. But tonight she had an ulterior motive.

'Of course,' she said.

She perched on the end of the bed. Finlay, under the covers now, turned the pages of his book to find out where he was, frowning slightly as he did so.

'The last time Georgie was here, did she say anything to you?' Casey asked him.

'What sort of anything?' Finlay said distractedly.

'I don't know. Something about her plans. Where she might be going. What she might be thinking.'

Finlay made a face. He was obviously giving her question his whole attention now. 'Yes,' he said at last. 'She asked me if I could keep a secret.'

Casey's heart was in her mouth. Did Finlay hold the clue to Georgie's whereabouts? 'Oh. And what did you say?'

'I said no. I told her my mummy and daddy told me I wasn't allowed to have secrets with a grown-up.'

'Did you? You're quite right to have said that, of course.' Damn modern parenting! And damn Finlay for being the model son.

Finlay held out his book. 'Here I am. Chapter Fifteen. Read it, Mummy.'

Casey found it almost impossible to concentrate, but she persevered until she reached the end of the chapter. Then, planting a kiss on Finlay's head, she said that was enough for one night and now it was time to go to sleep. She'd got as far as the door when Finlay called her back.

'Mummy,' he said.

'Yes, dear?'

'Georgie didn't take any notice, you know.'

'How do you mean, love?' said Casey.

'Well,' said Finlay, 'what I mean is she told me her secret anyway.'

★ ★ ★

'I'll be an hour, max,' Casey informed Dom when she came downstairs.

He'd just poured himself glass of wine and was midway through pouring another for her. She glanced at it wistfully. It would have been nice to curl up on the settee with a drink in front of the TV. But duty called.

'Have I missed something?' A perplexed Dom watched while Casey slipped her feet into her outdoor shoes before grabbing her bag and rummaging inside for her car keys.

'No,' she said. 'But it looks as if *I* might have. I'm off to see Georgie's parents. I think there's something they're not telling us.'

Mrs Spencer answered the door. She'd obviously been drinking. Her colour was high, and her voice as she demanded to know what Casey could possibly want at this time of night was louder than usual. Not that Casey blamed her. Knowing what she suspected now, thanks to Finlay's recent revelation, she'd have been blotto by six o'clock.

'I wonder if I could step inside?' Casey

asked her. 'I'd rather not talk about this on the doorstep.'

Mrs Spencer peered out into the night, her face half in shadow, half illuminated by the lamp in the porch.

'My husband's not in,' she said.

'All the better,' said Casey grimly.

★　★　★

'That didn't take long.'

A glance at the clock told Casey she'd been less than half an hour. Just long enough to be told that her son had a very vivid imagination and that if it was accepted practice nowadays to take the word of an eight-year-old boy over that of the victim's mother, then the criminal justice system was in a much worse way than she'd thought. Long enough too for Casey to reply that, actually, she was no longer sure that there *was* or ever *had* been a victim. And that's when she'd been shown the door.

'Michelle's been round,' Dom said. 'Something about a specialist rug cleaner. Said she'll take it in for you as it's en route to where she'll be tomorrow.'

Casey wasn't really listening. 'Did you give it to her?' she asked him, grabbing her glass and slumping down on the settee next to him.

'That's just it. I couldn't find it.'

She told him it was under the bed in the spare room. She'd drop it off tomorrow.

'You'll have to be quick,' Dom said. 'She said something about a course and an early start.'

Casey took a big gulp of wine. That was better.

'She said something else too. About one of her pupils. She thought this kid should speak to you.'

'Do you know what it was about?'

Dom shook his head. 'She seemed quite keen for you to talk to him, though.'

Casey heaved herself out of the settee. 'I'd better pop round now, before it gets any later.'

On went the outdoor shoes again.

'Hey! Don't forget the rug!' Dom shouted after her. 'You might as well kill two birds with one stone.'

But Casey had already left.

★ ★ ★

Omar had been off sick with a virus that wouldn't go away, he told Casey, which was why he hadn't come forward till now with what he knew. He sat across the desk from her in the small private office the school secretary had put them into for their 'little chat', as she'd called it.

He looked so earnest in his black-framed glasses and neat haircut, his uniform exactly as prescribed by the school with no attempt made at customising it. He was an 'A-star' student, so Michelle had told her — the go-to kid if you were stuck on your maths homework, and as honest, reliable and discreet as the day was long. He'd also been one of Georgie's closest confidantes since the beginning of the new academic year, when they'd found themselves in the same tutor group.

'It's just that when I saw those pictures of Georgie with Matt Ferrie and realised the implication, I knew I had to come forward and say something,' he said. 'It just didn't seem fair on her.'

'Because?'

'Do I need to spell it out?' Omar said. 'Him and her? It's just ridiculous. They were in different leagues.'

He'd expressed simply what Casey herself had thought the first time Matt's connection with Georgie had been brought to her attention. Why had she continued to go along with it? she wondered. Was it because there'd been no one else in the frame, and the nice girl who'd fallen for the bad boy had always been a convenient label to attach to a case such as this since time immemorial?

'So there was nothing between them?'

'She tried him out for a while but she soon got tired of him. No intellect, she said. And besides, she couldn't go out with anybody who wasn't a feminist.'

'She told you that?' She'd lay odds that Omar was a feminist. And that he was madly in love with Georgie too.

'Yes. Then *he* got in touch with her. The man who'd fathered her. She dropped Matt like a hot brick after that.'

So when Finlay had called her back to his side and repeated what Georgie had told him in confidence, he'd been telling the truth; that Georgie had made plans to visit her father. Her real one, Finlay said, and not Dr Spencer, who was, according to Finlay at least, only a pretend one. Admittedly they'd got a bit sidetracked while Casey explained the difference between a biological father and a father who'd brought you up. But when she'd asked him to repeat what he'd told her, he stuck to it, and she hadn't doubted him. She continued to believe him even after Mrs Spencer had accused him of having a fanciful imagination. And now that Omar had seconded Finlay's words, there was even less room for doubt.

Casey had so many questions for Omar. Had Georgie said how her father had managed to find her? Had she said anything about who he was or where he lived? Did he know if she'd even been aware of his existence before he'd got in touch?

'She said he made the first contact online.'

'Facebook?'

Omar gave her a disdainful look.

Apparently nobody under the age of twenty used Facebook anymore.

'OK.' Casey was suitably chastened. 'Did she tell you his name?'

'Not in so many words.'

'What do you mean by that?'

'Well, she showed me this photo of him from the *Brockhaven Gazette*.'

Casey sat bolt upright. Now they were getting somewhere!

'She'd had it in her bag for a while, I think. She'd folded it up small so when she unfolded it, it wouldn't lie flat.' He glanced at Casey apologetically. 'It was really hard to make him out with all the creases.'

'Just describe what you saw, Omar.'

'It was a bunch of people in a field. You know, that one out Endeby way? I think I recognised one of the people in it.'

'You mean you knew his name?'

'I think he's called Giles Seddon.'

★   ★   ★

Casey was back at the office, head down, madly googling for anything that might throw up a connection between Giles Seddon and Alex Spencer. Were they similar in age? she wondered. It seemed as if they might be. He was fifty; she was a couple of years younger. There was no university connection, so whatever had happened between them had started here, locally.

Had they both lived in this area for the same length of time and met each other at the same functions? Or was there a 'good cause' that had brought them together? Alex Spencer loved a good cause, and Giles Seddon loved to be associated with one, if it would raise his standing in a community where half the people who lived here were of the opinion that he was a money-grabbing so-and-so with designs on ripping up the blueprint for the English countryside in order to line his own pockets.

Jody Bright was sitting in the desk next to hers, squinting at her screen, blatantly trying to find out what she was doing. If she got any nearer, she'd be sitting on the same chair. You had to hand it to Jody; she didn't seem to be holding a grudge.

Already she'd asked about the case and how it was going, and made some observations about the pictures of Georgie and Matt that were in circulation, hoping they'd soon bring a result. Casey had replied as little as necessary. Call her small-minded, but she still hadn't really forgiven Jody for the way she'd tried to throw suspicion on Dom for Georgie's disappearance, wasting so much precious time into the bargain.

Gail came striding towards her, ignoring Jody's greeting. It was obvious she felt the same as Casey as far as Jody went. She was waving a bit of paper that looked like it might have been important.

'Casey,' she said, 'I've got Brighton police on the phone. Matt Ferrie's turned himself in.'

'Matt Ferrie has nothing to do with Georgie's disappearance,' Casey said.

'Really?' Jody glanced from Casey to Gail then back to Casey again. 'But I thought you said . . .'

Casey ignored her and took the piece of paper from Gail's outstretched hand.

'That's just what he said,' Gail replied.

'They've just faxed this through. His statement. Last time he saw her was last July at school, he said. He's been in Brighton since, working. And he's got more alibis than the Pope at a papal blessing.'

'We need to take his photo down,' Casey said, 'before he thinks about suing us.'

Now Gail was staring at Casey's computer screen. Casey had clicked on the *Brockhaven Gazette*'s website and was scrolling through the news items connected with the site at Endeby. The first thing that popped up was the picture she guessed Georgie must have shown Omar.

'Poor Giles Seddon,' Jody said. 'I feel sorry for that guy.'

Casey studied Seddon's face. There he stood, arms folded, staring at the camera, his chin jutting out defiantly. Could it really be that this was Georgie's father? She peered at his face for any similarities between him and Georgie.

She'd know Georgie a couple of years now. She was a kind, sweet, warm-hearted girl. She was vegetarian and had even spoken about becoming a vegan, 'to save the planet' as she'd put it. What she hated most of all was corporate greed. What on earth could she possibly have in common with Giles Seddon?

While her mind turned over all these things, Casey was mildly aware of a backwards and forwards exchange going on between Jody and Gail, who seemed to be having a bit of a disagreement about the protesters. Gail hoped Seddon wouldn't get his way over the holiday cottages. Jody thought differently.

'That land belongs to him,' Jody said. 'You should see what they've done to it. Wrecked it. I was down there yesterday trying to keep the peace between him and that other one. The one who brought all the others here in the first place. *He's* the one with all the groupies, hanging on to his every word.'

Casey turned her head away from the screen. What — or rather who — was Jody pointing at? She looked back at the photo. It occurred to her she'd been so caught up with Giles Seddon that she hadn't thought to look too closely at the other people surrounding him. But now she did.

They were a motley crew, young and old, men and women. There were plenty sporting the usual alternative dress code — the recycled tie-dyed pants and dresses, the tattoos and braids and piercings. But middle England was well represented at this protest too. The middle-aged women haranguing Seddon with their raised fists while he stood by and coolly ignored them wouldn't have looked out of place at a meeting of the Mothers' Union.

'Look at him!' Jody said, still continuing to jab her finger in the direction of the screen. 'Calls himself Dengo Hartley.'

Casey followed Jody's gaze. She had him in her sight now. And oh my God, the resemblance to Georgie was striking.

'Of course, he's just as well-connected as Giles Seddon,' Jody went on. 'I doubt he'd be able to do what he does, going round the country with his little entourage protesting here and protesting there, if he didn't have private means.'

He presumably was Dengo Hartley. She'd googled him now. Son of an earl. Christened Denholm. Not surprising you'd want to change a name like that to something a bit more street.

'Shut up, Jody,' Gail suddenly said. 'Casey's thinking.'

Jody surprised her by actually doing as she was told.

'Jody,' Casey said, 'when did you last pay the camp a visit?'

'Yesterday,' she said.

'And did you have a look round?'

'Not really. I didn't have time. *He* was too busy complaining about his damn cat.'

'Cat? What cat?'

It was an opportunity for Jody to take centre stage, and she made the most of it. Apparently there'd been an accusation from Dengo Hartley that Giles Seddon had killed his cat.

'He said it was just the kind of malicious thing he'd do to hurt him because he knew how attached he was to it.'

Gail snorted. Casey said nothing.

Could it be the same cat as the one Dom had run over? Well, it was in the right place, she guessed. It could easily have run out of the camp and under Dom's wheels.

'I know it sounds like a joke, Gail,' an irate Jody said. 'But honestly, at one point I thought I might have to call for backup. I had to put myself between them or it could have got nasty.'

Casey decided it was high time she butted in. 'So you didn't see a girl who resembled Georgie Spencer so much that it might, in fact, have been her?' she said.

Jody wrinkled her brow. Casey kept her eyes on her, willing Jody to remember. It was futile. After several long moments of watching Jody struggle to put together the pieces of her previous afternoon, she gave up waiting.

'That's where she is, you know,' she announced. 'And I'm going to go and bring her home.'

But first, she needed to pay a call on the Spencers. She'd finally understood why the atmosphere in that house had been so toxic on her last visit. Neither of them were mourning Georgie. Because they both knew that Georgie was and never had been in any danger. Perhaps what they had been in mourning for was the death of their marriage.

★ ★ ★

Once more, Casey was informed that Dr Spencer wasn't at home. It was obviously a struggle for him to remain under the same roof as his wife.

'We need to talk,' Casey said on the doorstep. 'Woman to woman. Let me in, please.'

Mrs Spencer led her into the drawing room and gestured for Casey to take a seat.

'Don't you think it's about time you started telling the truth, Alex?' Casey said.

Mrs Spencer's eyes strayed to the half-empty bottle on the coffee table.

'I'm sorry,' she said at last. 'I've wasted police time. But I had to keep it a secret. Don't you see?'

'Dengo Hartley is Georgie's father,'

Casey said. 'Somehow she found out.'

'He contacted her. Don't ask me how. I don't understand how social media works. It seems to change every other month.'

She'd known as early as the next morning, when Georgie texted her to say that Hartley had picked her up at a pre-arranged venue and taken her to the protest site. But she couldn't say anything.

'How could I tell my husband he wasn't Georgie's father after all?'

'I'm guessing he knows now, though,' Casey said,

Mrs Seddon nodded, tears streaming down her face. Casey didn't really want to know the story behind Alex Spencer's fling with Dengo Hartley. But she heard it anyway. It was about as sordid as these things usually were. Dr Hartley, working all the hours God sent trying to make a name for the GP practice he'd staked all his ambitions on. She, married less than two years when she met Dengo Hartley socially. She'd thought him idealistic and passionate, she said. It hadn't lasted long.

'The truth is that Dengo Hartley cares no more about the planet than the likes of Giles Seddon,' she said. 'He cares more for the publicity and the groupies.'

Groupies. Wasn't that how Jody described them, the women of all ages who flocked around him, thrilled to be part of his inner circle? Thinking of Jody, she was going to have to stop acting like such a cow towards her. After all, hadn't she been just as suspicious of Dom herself — a man she'd taken a vow to stick with through thick and thin? There was the small detail of Jody pointing her gaze in the right direction too, away from Seddon and towards Hartley. It might have taken her a bit longer to get there herself if she hadn't had Jody's assistance.

'All I can hope is that Georgie sees through the veneer. He'll grow tired of her soon enough. A pretty daughter can only give him so much mileage. When he realises what being a father really means, he'll drop her like a hot potato.'

'Do you want me to go and fetch her?' Casey asked.

'More than anything in the world. I just wish you could bring my husband back to me too.'

★　★　★

Casey pulled up outside the Spencers' once more. Persuading Georgie to come home had taken no time at all. She'd practically thrown herself in the back of the car as soon Casey opened the door without so much as a backward glance at Dengo Hartley, who was more concerned that he wouldn't be had up for child abduction than saying goodbye to the daughter with whom he'd only just been reunited. Casey told him she wasn't promising anything.

After one single ring of the doorbell, the door was flung open, and Mrs Spencer wrapped her arms round Georgie.

'I'm so sorry, mum,' Georgie said. 'It was stupid of me. I only wanted to see what he was like.'

And now you have, thought Casey.

'Where's dad?' said Georgie when she

was finally allowed to extricate herself from her mother's grasp.

Poor Georgie. She was bright, intelligent. She looked like a woman. But she was a girl; an adolescent. And like most adolescents, she was the centre of her world — ill-equipped to understand the devastation she'd set in motion; the collapse of the world inhabited by the two people she loved best after herself.

But maybe Casey was wrong. Because coming out of the shadows of the hallway came Dr Spencer. He looked tired and pale, but when he saw Georgie he went straight to her and hugged her just as hard as Mrs Spencer had. 'I'm here,' he said.

Casey walked away then, back to her car. She didn't know the ending of this story. She just hoped it would be a happy one. She was an optimist. She'd seen the pride in Dr Spencer's eyes when Georgie had called him Dad. It was obvious that in his eyes, Georgie was his daughter still. Whether or not Mrs Spencer was still his wife was another matter.

'Casey!'

Georgie was calling her name. She turned round to find out what she wanted.

'Do you still need a babysitter?' Georgie asked.

Casey smiled and gave a nod of her head. 'I'll give you a call,' she said.

A HOUSE TO DIE FOR

'Laura, have you seen my car keys?'

Will's voice floated down the stairs. Why was her husband so convinced she knew where to lay her hands on everything he mislaid during the course of one day? Was it because she was a detective constable, so looking for stuff — be it stolen goods, criminals, or missing persons — was part of her job?

Breathe, Laura told herself. *Think of the baby*. There was a hormone, wasn't there, that pregnant women released? It was meant to turn you into an unflappable ruminant, slow to anger and totally indifferent to the small irritations of everyday life. Well, all she could say was it seemed to have bypassed her.

He was back in the kitchen now, presumably having given up looking for his keys upstairs. He scanned the room vaguely, which was what passed for looking in Will's book. A sudden series of thumps from Tillie's room directly over-head startled both of them.

'What on earth's she doing up there?'

'Same as you,' Laura said. 'Looking for something. It's PE today and she can't find her shorts.'

And to think she still had a full day's work ahead of her — sitting at a desk in charge of every file marked 'Boring' while her fellow officers got their teeth into the juicy stuff. Just because she was pregnant. Fine, she could see the logic of keeping her and her yet-to-be-born baby out of the way of dangerous criminals. But she still had a brain, didn't she?

Wearily, she transferred a pile of magazines from the nearest chair to the table so she could sit down for a moment. The sound of tinkling keys falling to the floor made her start.

'Did you hear that?' Will, who was as lithe and limber as Laura was lumbering, bent to retrieve them. 'And look what else was down there!' He held Tillie's lost shorts aloft triumphantly.

'I must have dropped them when I was sorting out the laundry.'

'You look tired, love,' Will said. 'We should get Mum here to help. You know she'd love to.'

'And you know I'd love to have her. But where would we put her?'

The spare room was bursting at the seams with junk. At the last count it contained two broken desktop computers, a chair with a wobbly leg that Will had promised to mend but hadn't quite got round to yet, a number of suitcases of varying dimensions, and several piles of books neither of them could bear to part with.

There was another bang from upstairs.

'Goodness!' Laura cried. 'I forgot all about Tillie! Go and tell her we've found her shorts, will you, love? And say that if she wants a lift from me, I'm leaving in exactly five minutes.'

Her eye caught the front page of the *Havensea Weekly News* and lingered over the headlines. 'PROPERTY SECTION INSIDE', it said. Grabbing it, she stuffed it in her bag. What harm would there be in looking? Four bedrooms, a bigger garden. Perhaps even a granny annexe. Laura's mood had suddenly brightened. New baby, new home. *Why not*, she thought, springing from her chair with the energy of a woman with a plan.

★   ★   ★

This would be the longest period of time that Carole had been back in Havensea in thirty-five years. Normally her visits were shorter. Three days at Christmas, when she barely left the house. Then Dad's birthday in July, when she'd whisk him away for a few days somewhere in the UK once he started finding flights to see her in Tenerife too difficult. But now she would be back in Havensea just as summer was beginning. Long days, short nights. Always looking over her shoulder. Just in case.

She hated having to live at Dad's. The house was small, dark and poky, and since his stroke — the reason for her flying back in the first place — he'd moved downstairs, taking up the whole of the living room, which meant the TV had to go off and she was forced to disappear

202

into her bedroom at ten. It was no life for a woman used to her own light and airy apartment in a country where the evenings usually began round about midnight. But as things stood, she was just going to have to grin and bear it.

On the fifth night of her stay, Carole sat staring into space, wondering how she was going to get through the rest of the evening. To think people came to Havensea on holiday. Families, pensioners, couples on day trips. They'd parade along the sea front, walk up and down the pier, have a go at the slot machines, and queue for fish and chips.

When the weather was fine — and in a British summer you could pretty well count the days they would be on the fingers of one hand — they'd sit outside The Red Lion and watch the world go by, deluding themselves that when the sun shone and the temperature hit double figures, there was no better place on earth to spend your summer holiday than good old Havensea.

'You want to get a job.'

Dad's words broke the silence. She

struggled to understand him at first. Not just because the TV was on far too loud as usual, but because since the stroke, Dad's speech had become difficult for her to understand.

'Don't be silly,' she replied when she'd finally understood him. 'I'm here to look after you. How can I get a job?'

Though already his suggestion was taking seed. Thanks to social services, who appeared to have successfully divided up Dad's week between two carers and the local day centre, she was beginning to feel more or less redundant. It seemed to Carole that the carers knew far more about her father than she, his own flesh and blood, did these days. Of the two, she greatly preferred Ollie, who was on his gap year and saving up to go travelling before he went to university. He was polite and respectful, both to Dad and to herself, and he didn't drone on about his troubles like the other carer, Mona, did.

It struck Carole that Mona was obviously under the impression that this was her house and that things would run a great deal more smoothly if she herself wasn't here. Already she'd had words with her for smoking in the back garden, which hadn't gone down well. Not that Carole gave a hoot. Mona might be able to run rings round Dad, but Carole was immune.

It wasn't only the carers to whom she'd relinquished her responsibilities either. On two mornings a week and on three afternoons, Dad was out of the house at the day centre, which left Carole home alone twiddling her thumbs. Thinking about it, she certainly had time to do a job. And she could definitely do with the money.

Alfredo, for whom she'd worked selling holiday properties for the last fifteen years, had agreed to keep her position open, but he'd said nothing about paying her in her absence. She still had to pay the mortgage on her little flat even though she wasn't living in it, and her savings wouldn't last forever.

'There's a job come up at your old place,' Dad, who was in an expansive mood this evening, said. 'You used to like it at Taberner and Driscoll's.'

'Up to a point,' she conceded.

'We thought you was going to stay there, your mum and me. Least till you got married. You had security. Then you went running off over the sea for no reason.'

Oh, there'd been a reason all right. Though not one she'd ever wanted to share with her parents. 'Let's not bring all that up again, Dad,' she said. 'I've no regrets. And I was never going to meet Mr Right stuck in a poky little estate agent's on the high street.'

'He was sweet on you, wasn't he, though? That lad who worked there with you.'

'Who? You mean George Corker? I'm surprised you remember him. I haven't thought about him in years.'

In fact, she could barely remember what he looked like. He appeared to her now as an amalgam of various components. A fine sprinkling of dandruff on the shoulders of his ill-fitting suit, a sweaty forehead speckled with pimples, stubby fingers with bitten nails, feet that bumped into the furniture whenever he moved.

'Trouble with you is, you had ideas above your station, my girl. We were never good enough for you once you started that babysitting job up at the big house.'

The muscles in her neck felt suddenly tense. 'Dad, please. All that was a long time ago. Tell me about this job.' Anything to distract him.

'I don't remember. It was Ollie who brought it up when I told him about you.'

'What do you mean, when you told him about me?' she snapped. 'Just *what* did you tell him, exactly?'

'Keep your hair on. Anybody'd think you had something to hide. I just mentioned you'd worked there when you left school. That's what jogged his memory. Said he'd seen an advert in the window there.'

Carole apologised. The last thing she wanted was an atmosphere. To appease him, she promised to have a look. 'I don't suppose it can do any harm,' she said.

Her father nodded, seemingly satisfied. But he hadn't finished with her yet. 'He's still there, you know. Martin Boulton. Up in that big house all on his own. The White House, wasn't that its name? Don't know what happened to the other one, though.'

'Who? Adam?'

Dad sniggered. 'Bit of a habit up there, folk disappearing.'

Carole picked up the remote and pointed it at the TV. She'd had more than enough of this conversation.

★　★　★

Laura was meant to be reading through the applications for her maternity leave cover so that she could offer up an opinion on the most suitable candidate. Only, she was struggling with the idea of another person doing her job. What if they were better than her? Or if people liked the cover more than they liked her and decided they didn't want her to come back? So she was putting off the evil hour by looking through all the houses for sale on Taberner and Driscoll's website.

Ravi Hasheed, who'd not long qualified as a PC, so hadn't yet reached the point in his career when the last thing he wanted to do at the end of a long night shift was to hang around making small talk with the day shift, was keeping her company. Between them, they'd already passed an opinion on every house within Laura's price range. Now they were checking out the properties they'd never be able to afford even in their wildest dreams.

'Sadly, my very favourite house doesn't appear to be for sale,' she said.

'Which one's that?' Ravi asked her.

'That big white one on the sea front. Three floors, balcony, big garden. Funny turrets running round it. The White House, I think it's called. Reminds me of something from an Agatha Christie story.'

'Ah, that one!'

Ravi's reaction — as if he knew something she didn't — provoked her interest. 'Come on, Ravi,' she teased, 'tell me what you know!'

'If you want the lowdown, you need to speak to my mum. She did some nursing up there when she first qualified.'

Ravi came from a family of medics. As

well as his mum, his father was a surgeon up at the county hospital. Ravi had been a disappointment to them, he often said, becoming a police officer instead of following the family tradition like his older siblings had. If he'd become a doctor instead of joining the police, he was fond of grumbling, he'd be able to afford his own flat now, instead of still having to live at home with his parents at the age of twenty-four.

'If I remember rightly, Mum got to know Mrs Boulton — Margot, I think she was called — when she began nursing her husband. They kept in touch when he died. I think they had a lot in common. Two grande dames, if you know what I mean.'

Laura did. She'd once given Ravi a lift home and had been invited in to meet the family. As soon as she'd set eyes on Ravi's mother, she'd thought there was something regal about her. Even at three in the afternoon, she'd been exquisitely dressed; and she'd been the epitome of good manners, pressing tea and cake on Laura as if there was nothing she wanted more than to spend the next hour with her.

'Anyway, she met some other bloke within months and got engaged. But then he went missing.'

'How do you mean?'

'Mysteriously like,' Ravi said. 'There was a search, enquiries, everything. But he's never been found, dead or alive. Case is still open, probably. According to my mum, Margot Boulton was loyal to the end. Swore he'd never have left her of his own volition.'

This story just got better and better. 'You mean she thought he'd been murdered?' Laura said, aghast.

Ravi nodded and yawned at the same time. He was going to have to go home and get some kip or he'd be fit for nothing, he said. But Laura didn't even hear him go. She was already looking up the number of the *Havensea Gazette*. If this story had made the news, then she would very much like to see a picture of the glamorous Margot Boulton and read up on the details Ravi had missed out. Let the super choose her replacement. She'd far rather get stuck into some proper detective work.

Five minutes later, she had her article. There they were, the two lovers. Margot with her Princess Diana haircut and her pussy-bow dress, gazing up adoringly at her handsome beau with his floppy hair and his wide lapels. What had really happened to him back then? she wondered. Was it really a straightforward choice between two alternatives, as the police had stated? Had he fled abroad because he owed money, or because the idea of marrying Margot Boulton, a woman older than him by a good few years, had lost its appeal? Or had something more sinister occurred?

★ ★ ★

It was her job to sell this house, but in order to sell it, first she had to acquaint herself with its smells and its sounds. Carole loved this bit best: that moment when she turned the key in the front door, crossed over the threshold, and then stood there, alone in an empty house, tuning into its heartbeat.

They'd snapped her up at Taberner and Driscoll's, like she'd known they would. The job was part-time and temporary, since the previous incumbent had gone off on sick leave. No one knew if the woman she'd replaced would be coming back soon or at all. Either way, it suited Carole. If it was the former, then she'd just have to find something else. If the latter, then she'd stay as long as she could. That way she could at least keep an eye on that Mona Reardon.

At the interview, it had come as a huge surprise to discover that George Corker, her erstwhile suitor, not only still worked here but had been promoted to manager. Thankfully, he'd changed for the better. Gone were the shiny forehead, the pimples and the dandruff. His hair had turned steel-grey, but he still had plenty of it. And someone had given him a few lessons on how to dress — a wife, maybe; though there was no sign of a wedding ring.

His manner had been less awkward too. Though in retrospect that was probably because he'd had time to deal with whatever old feelings he'd had about her. Either that, or he'd forgotten all about her just as she'd forgotten all about him till Dad had thrown his name into the conversation.

'I've taken over Janey's workload as much as I can,' he said as the interview drew to a close. 'But already I'm drowning. The owners of a house on Marlborough Close rang this morning. Just before you arrived, in fact. They need to move fast. How soon can you get round there to value it?'

'The job's mine, then?' she said.

'If you can do this right away, then yes.'

Of course she'd accepted with no hesitation. Though she'd lied about being able to do the valuation immediately. She'd promised Dad fish and chips for lunch and she didn't want to break her word. But luck was on her side. The roads were empty and there'd been no queue at the chippy. She'd grabbed a single portion of haddock and chips, resisting for herself, and sped home just as Ollie was leaving. When she announced she'd got the job at the estate agent's but that she was in a mad rush to do a valuation in Marlborough Close, he'd taken the fish and chips from her and told her he'd sort out Dad's lunch. It didn't matter if he was held up, as unlike her, he had no other plans, he said.

'Bless you, Ollie!' she'd said, before waving goodbye to Dad and fleeing.

So now she was here at number five. It was one of the new four-bedroomed houses on the new estate. Her first impression was of a stylish interior. She guessed the present owners were well-heeled, and either childless or empty-nesters. She spent some time examining the framed photos sitting on the Scandi-cool, expensive-looking console in the hall, trying to work out the relationship between the people in them, before moving quietly round the house, taking photos and checking the dimensions of the various rooms.

After about an hour of this, when she'd been upstairs and down several times, she took a seat at the table by the living room window to check a few facts online. Schools, transport links, all the things that could either clinch a deal in moments or put someone off just as quickly.

She soon became engrossed in her search. But as she clicked from one site to another, she gradually became aware of movement. It had been her understanding that the owners were abroad on holiday. Had they come back unexpectedly? When she thought she heard a footstep on the stairs, she froze.

'Hello?' she called out, but there was no answer.

Yes, there it went again. Was that the front door closing? She jumped to her feet, but in her rush to get a view outside, she stubbed her toe on the heavy coffee table. By the time she'd limped to the window, there was nothing to be seen.

If there had been anyone here, then she didn't think they were here any longer. Cautiously, her laptop under one arm for protection, she crept into the hallway. She'd never been of a nervous disposition, nor did she believe in ghosts. But right now, a ghost would have been far more acceptable than a silent intruder.

Her eye was immediately drawn to the photos on the console she'd examined earlier. Something was different. That photograph. Where had it come from? The woman, tall, elegant, dressed in the fashion of the time. The man, younger, pop-star looks.

She recognised the couple immediately. It was Margot. And him. Lawrence Chambers. She closed her eyes, her heart beating in wild terror. She had to get out of here right away. Grabbing her mac slung over the bannister, Carole yanked open the door and fled down the path.

★ ★ ★

If Laura had felt that her talents were being put to better use, she probably would have lost interest in Lawrence Chambers as quickly as the police obviously had. As far as they were concerned, he'd either got himself mixed up in some dodgy dealings and had fled abroad, or he'd grown disenchanted with Margot Boulton and struck out for pastures new before she could get that ring on her finger.

But she still had two weeks left before she went off on maternity leave, and her current shifts were killing her with boredom. What could possibly be wrong with doing some secret sleuthing of her own? And when she realised the mobile lying on her desk belonged to Ravi, who in his exhaustion must have forgotten it, she decided that Fate had lent a hand.

The case was still open even thirty-six years after Lawrence Chambers had disappeared. If she could unearth some evidence that foul play had been involved in his disappearance, then what was to say she couldn't persuade the super to let her have another look at it? And where better to start than with Ravi's mum?

She scrawled through Ravi's contact list till she arrived at 'Mum' and dialled. Mrs Hasheed answered her mobile immediately. Even better, she was at home. It would be absolutely no trouble at all to drop Ravi's phone round to the house, Laura said when Mrs Hasheed said she mustn't think of putting herself out, and that anyway, it might do Ravi good to be without it for a few hours, since he spent far too much time on it in her opinion.

'I'll be there in ten minutes,' Laura replied.

Fifteen minutes later, she was comfortably ensconced in a fireside chair in Mrs Hasheed's lounge, putting her feet up at Mrs Hasheed's insistence, enjoying a lovely cup of tea and plotting how she could bring up the topic of Margot Boulton and her missing boyfriend without it sounding too obvious that this was the main purpose of her visit.

In the end, she was actually rather proud of how skilfully she segued from the topic of forgetful sons and daughters (Ravi and Tillie respectively), to new babies and the current lack of space at Laura's house versus the abundance of lovely space at the Hasheeds'. From there it was but a hop, skip and jump before Laura divulged that she and her husband were looking to move and that in fact that evening the two of them would be sitting down to take a look at the latest listings and booking some viewing appointments.

And that no doubt in the end they'd end up in a four-bedroomed new build on one of the estates, which would probably be fine but not a patch on the kind of house she'd always dreamed of owning.

'That one — The White House. Now that's my favourite. Do you know it? Just a bit up from the sea front. 1920s, I think. Beautiful!'

'Appearances can be very deceptive, my dear,' Mrs Hasheed said. 'I'm not sure that house is a very happy one.'

'Oh? Why's that?'

'My friend lived there. Well, we weren't friends initially. I'd just started nursing. Her husband was my first private patient.'

Laura reached for a biscuit from the plate Mrs Hasheed held out.

'She and I became close during the period of his illness despite the fact that she was a great deal older than me,' Mrs Hasheed continued. 'Margot Boulton was her name.' She felt sorry for her, Mrs Hasheed said, left with two boys the way she had been. 'I felt she leaned on me for support. She was a timid woman, you see. Let those boys run rings round her.'

'She didn't have any other help?'

'Not what you'd call real help. A woman to do the cleaning. A local girl to babysit Adam, the younger one. Though in the end that ended rather badly, as I remember.'

Laura pricked up her ears. In what way? she asked. Mrs Hasheed looked suddenly embarrassed.

'Well, I don't like to spread gossip,' she said. 'And anyway, it was a long time ago. But I think the girl got involved with Martin, the older boy. Margot found them in bed together. In *her* bed, if you please.'

'So that was the end of that,' Laura said. 'It must have been hard for her.'

'Yes. She was often in tears because of some misdemeanour one or the other had committed. Could never stand up to them.'

'Were they that bad?'

Mrs Hasheed shrugged. Perhaps if their father hadn't been the invalid he was for most of their lives, then maybe they'd have turned out differently, she said. 'But as it was, they were either indulged or ignored, and nothing in between. I nursed Margot's husband for three years until 1980. Martin was at university for much of that time and Adam was away at boarding school.'

Laura was desperate to get to the new lover. Taking the bull by the horns, she suggested that Margot Boulton must have been lonely after her husband died, with her two sons away for most of the year.

'Funny you should say that,' Mrs Hasheed said. 'In fact she met someone else quite quickly. Lawrence Chambers, he was called. Ten years younger than her, he was.'

'A toyboy!'

Mrs Hasheed look pained. 'I suppose so.'

'What was he like?'

'I hardly knew him. She didn't seem to want to show him off much. Not to me, at least.'

There was a photograph of Ravi's mum as a young woman on the mantelpiece. She was wearing a beautiful sari and looked absolutely ravishing. Hardly surprising that Margot Boulton preferred to keep her younger boyfriend under wraps.

'He was some sort of dealer. Wine, antiques, I'm not sure which. Very handsome. She adored him. Trouble is, the boys didn't.' Margot would phone her at all times of the day and night, she said, in tears. 'So many rows. They wanted her to give him up. But she wouldn't. In fact, only three months into their relationship, she announced they were going to get married.'

'I bet that went down well.'

'The rows got worse. There were actual physical fights, and on at least one occasion Margot had to pull one or other of the boys off Lawrence.'

And then, apparently, Lawrence Chambers disappeared.

'That was when Margot stopped calling me.'

'You lost touch? You'd think at a time like that a friend was the one thing she'd need most.'

'I don't know what happened,' Mrs Hasheed said. 'I tried to get in touch once I read in the paper that there was a search going on for Lawrence. But it was always one of the boys who answered.' It was as if Margot were deliberately avoiding her, Mrs Hasheed said.

'Why would she do that?'

Mrs Hasheed took off her glasses and rubbed them with a cloth for a long time, as if deliberating whether or not to risk saying any more. Laura felt a prickle of excitement run through her. The thing to do now was to keep quiet, not to interrupt and to let Mrs Hasheed do the talking. Because Laura sensed that whatever came out of Mrs Hasheed's mouth next had a great deal of significance.

'I think she told me too much,' she said at last, and replaced her specs back on her nose. 'And she was afraid I might draw my own conclusions.'

'What sort of conclusion?'

'That one of the boys — or both — had killed him.'

★   ★   ★

There would be no getting out of hosting this open viewing. Carole realised that as soon as she showed George the photos of number 5, Marlborough Close back at the office. This place would sell fast, he'd told her. And it would sell high too, if they got a bunch of couples all round at the same time.

'You just watch. They'll claw each other's eyes out to get the keys to this place,' he said.

She'd imagined that he would want to take charge of the viewing himself, given how excited he appeared to be. But no. It was her baby, he said, smiling at her fondly in a way that alarmed her. She'd done all the hard work, so she should be the one to take the credit when it came to closing a deal. So not only was she forced to go back into that house again but, it looked like George's teenage crush had been reawakened. She didn't know which was worse.

At least this time she wouldn't have to go there alone. The viewing was fixed for Saturday afternoon at three p.m. Within an hour of the description going online, interest had been shown by six couples. There was safety in numbers, wasn't that what people said?

Four couples were already waiting for her outside the house as she drew up, five minutes before the agreed time. Another couple arrived just as she was introducing herself. While waiting for the final couple, she spent a long time extolling the virtues of the house exterior.

When one or two began to look at their watches and a third, less subtle, bluntly remarked that at this rate it would be sundown before they went inside, Carole realised she couldn't avoid it a moment longer. When the final couple turned up, there was no excuse to linger longer. They were accompanied by a girl, presumably their daughter, who Carole guessed to be probably round nine or ten years of age.

'I'm so sorry we're late,' the woman, who was heavily pregnant, said. 'I was held up at work.'

'Working at the weekends?' Carole raised her eyes in mock horror. 'Poor you! I thought it was only estate agents who did that.'

Pushing herself to the front of the group, the little girl piped up, 'My mummy's a detective. She has to work long hours to catch the criminals because they don't keep office hours.'

There was a ripple of amusement among the rest of the group and Carole joined in, fixing her brightest smile on her face. A police detective. That was all she needed.

'Right,' she trilled. 'Now that we're all here at last, let's go inside.'

★　★　★

Laura didn't know how the other couples felt, but she, for one, was distinctly miffed at the idea of wandering around somebody else's house in a big group like this. She didn't think Will liked it much, either. In fact, she got the distinct impression that he'd rather be anywhere but here on a Saturday afternoon.

He wasn't even sure they needed to move. What they really should be doing was getting rid of all the stuff they'd accumulated over the years, he'd said. In theory, she agreed. But it was just so difficult. It wasn't that she was a hoarder.

Just that she wasn't overly keen on throwing stuff away.

The people who lived in this house — where were they? she wondered — were obviously the opposite of hoarders. 'Minimalistic' was the word she'd overheard someone in the group use to describe it. 'Soulless' was the word Will had used when she'd relayed this description to him as they wandered out of the stainless-steel kitchen.

'Do you want to carry on looking?' Will whispered as they narrowly avoided another couple coming in.

'We haven't done upstairs yet,' she said, forgetting to whisper back.

'Let me take you up there,' the estate agent said. 'You can be the first while everyone else is still milling about down here.'

'Good-o,' Tillie, who was enjoying herself immensely, said.

Laura wished she could be as enthusiastic as her daughter. She knew the woman was only doing her job. But her manner had begun to irritate her within moments of entering the house. It seemed to her to be bordering on panicked. She couldn't seem to stop talking, falling over her words and flapping her hands about to make a point while her eyes darted round the room like she was expecting someone to jump out at her and shout 'boo'.

She sent Will a look that she hoped he'd read correctly. *Let's get this over with asap, then we can get out of here*, it said. He met her gaze and gave a nod so subtle anyone else would have missed it.

The small talk continued up the stairs. When was the baby due? Did they know what they were having? What about names, and was Laura okay on the stairs?

'And this is the master bedroom!'

The estate agent, wearing a badge with the name 'Carole Prescott' inscribed on it, flung open the door. It was another understated, elegantly furnished room where everything had been tidied away so as not to give so much as the slightest clue about the lives or personalities of the home owners. Everything bar one thing. Tillie, bounding over to the bed on which it lay, was the first to spot and claim it.

'Look at this!' she said, waving the object in front of their faces. 'It's a puppet.'

Tillie had inserted her small hand inside the body so now Laura was able to recognise that the puppet was a woman. It had shortish bright yellow hair dipping down over one eye, which gave it a coy expression, and it was wearing a bright red dress with a pussy-bow collar. She couldn't help thinking she'd seen a dress like that recently.

'Put it back, Tillie,' she said, with an apologetic glance at Carole Prescott, who for the first time since they'd first met was silent at last, her mouth drawn in a thin line and her face scarily white. She seemed unable to take her eyes away from the puppet.

'Oh dear,' Laura said. 'Are you all right?'

'No,' whispered the other woman. 'Actually, I think I'm going to faint.'

And those were the last words she said before she went crashing down to the floor.

* * *

It had been Ollie's suggestion to bring Dad down here in the wheelchair. At first she'd been dead set against the idea. How on earth was she going to manage Dad and a wheelchair on her own? Ollie might have been skinny, but he was a strong young man who'd had plenty of practice at lifting and manoeuvring the elderly. But the thought of being stuck inside for the whole of the bank holiday weekend when Dad's day care centre was closed convinced her he'd been right to suggest it. All that sea and sky and open air would be bound to help take her mind off things.

Except it hadn't. All she could think of was the puppet on the bed, the photograph, and the woman who was pictured there. Who had put them there? The more she thought about it, the more she came up with the same answer. It had to be George. He was the only person who knew she would be at that address. In fact, hadn't he sent her there on both occasions? Plus he was the only person with access. Apart from the owners of course. But when she'd asked him where they were, George had told her they were away on a fortnight's holiday somewhere in the Caribbean. How likely was it that they would be able to pop back to set her up, then disappear again?

So if it *was* George, what was his game? What if she'd totally misconstrued that glance of his back in the office yesterday, and it was something more sinister than admiration?

All the years she'd lived abroad, she'd been free of anxiety and had never felt the need to look over her shoulder all the time in the way she was doing now. The only way to put all this behind her was obviously to take the next flight back to Tenerife. But what about Dad?

She glanced down at him and gently inched his wheelchair further into the shade. He looked happy, licking his ice cream and waiting for the puppet show to start. Like an excited child. Tenderly, she bent over him to dab away some ice cream from the corner of his mouth. Funny, but even a week ago she couldn't have imagined herself doing something like this. Old age and sickness had always repelled her. But now, surrounded by all these other noisy holidaymakers, it seemed the most natural thing in the world. How could she leave him?

All around, the sound of happy anticipation grew. Even the seagulls gathered overhead, jostling each other and screeching their excitement as the moment for the show to begin grew closer.

'Are you ready, boys and girls?' the puppeteer shouted, to a great roar of 'yes' from the crowd. Carole, squatting on the step in the shade of Dad's wheelchair, rested her head against it and closed her eyes. She was overcome with drowsiness, exhausted with all the pushing and soothed by the atmosphere around her. If she could just close her eyes for a moment, she'd feel better, she told herself.

At first, she didn't know if she was awake or dreaming. Her throat was dry and she was no longer in the shade. The sun was hot on her face. She stared up at the stage, blinking a few times, trying to work out the scene that was playing out in front of her.

In the centre of the stage, a yellow-haired female puppet in a bright red dress was sobbing loudly. A second puppet, male this time, dressed as a groom, a top hat by his side, a spray in his buttonhole, lay at her feet.

'You've killed him! You've killed him!' she cried over and over again while the audience of children roared with laughter at her exaggerated grief. In the wings, two other puppets kept peeping round the curtain, then disappearing again almost immediately, to the roar of the children who yelled out their presence to the grieving woman who inevitably failed to spot them each time she looked around.

Carole was the only member of the audience not laughing. Instead she sat, horrified at what she'd seen. That puppet was the same one that had been lying on the bed in the master bedroom at the house in Marlborough Close and which the little girl had waved in her face. It was Margot. That Lady Di haircut. The dress with the pussy-bow neckline. Margot's hair. Margot's clothes.

How embarrassing, fainting like that.

'Isn't it me who's meant to pass out after walking up the stairs?' the pregnant detective had joked, handing her a bottle of water and fanning her with her copy of the house details.

And those boy puppets in the wings. One tall and dark — Martin, of course. The other shorter, carrot-topped. Adam. Adam the puppeteer. Adam the magician. Adam the wronged child, back to claim his due. Finally, she understood.

Dad appeared to be asleep, but when Carole took the brake off the wheelchair, he woke immediately.

'Where are we going now?' he muttered.

Carole, ignoring him, steered him along the promenade, bulldozing her way through the throng. Beneath the warm sun, she was sweating buckets. But she had to get away from this place immediately.

'Carole! Slow down, will you, girl. What's the big rush?'

'It's finished, Dad,' she panted. 'It's all over.'

Oh yes, it was all over all right. Ahead

she could see the ramp leading away from the beach up to the main road. On the way here, coming down had been a breeze. Going up threatened to be more of a struggle. But she barely gave it a moment's thought. It was as if she'd suddenly been endowed with superhuman strength. Aware of nothing but the widening distance between them and the ever disappearing coastline, she bumped and buffeted the wheelchair to the top.

Finally, they'd reached the road. With her eyes fixed straight ahead, she advanced across it. There was a sudden screech of brakes, a slamming door. Then there he stood, in front of her. Yelling. Gesticulating. What the hell did she think she was doing walking out into the road like that? And in charge of a wheelchair too! But then he stopped, dumbfounded.

'Carole!' he said. 'You!'

'Martin,' she replied.

★ ★ ★

The last thing he needed was a brush with the law or a spat with the Punch and

Judy guy whose spot he'd nicked. He'd already had one warning. He'd been promised a broken jaw if it happened again, and he believed it too. Seriously, the guy was a giant.

The theatre had taken no time at all to dismantle, but it was taking longer to pack away the props. He'd grown strangely fond of these puppets of his. There they lay, side by side on the pebbly beach. First her, with that yellow woollen hair, those spidery eyelashes, the full red lips. And then the blouse with the frilly bow. It was a pretty good copy of the one in the photo, even if he did say so himself. And you had to admire the work that had gone into the groom, with his top hat and tails and his twirling moustache.

Course, Lawrence Chambers had never had a twirling moustache, and his liaison with his mother had never actually got as far as a wedding. But if Carole Prescott had been at the show — and that message on his phone yesterday more than reassured him she had — then the likeness wouldn't have been lost on her.

And once she'd worked that out, she'd soon have worked out who the other three puppets were meant to be.

He'd wondered about hanging on to them. They'd taken him ages to make, and there was probably a good deal more mileage still left in them. But reason was telling him it was time to move on.

He dug his phone out from his jeans pocket and checked through his messages again, just in case he'd missed a new one. But there was nothing. Just the one from yesterday. 'Job done. She'll be there for the show.'

So far, so good. But now it was time for the next step. To make it known he meant business. He began his text. 'Just got one more favour to ask you, buddy,' he wrote before he pressed Send.

★ ★ ★

The White House hadn't changed much, in Carole's eyes. Maybe the stucco exterior was a little less white, the path leading up to the house a little crumblier and the garden — or what could be seen of it from the coastal path — a tad less well-maintained.

With her estate agent's hat on, there were things she would have done to lure in a passing prospective buyer. A couple of symmetrical bay trees set out on either side of the front door would have done the trick. And on closer inspection, the front door, imposing though it was, would have benefited from a fresh coat of paint. But she wasn't here to sell the place.

The bottle had been the first thing Martin reached for once he let her inside. Not her hand. Nor her cheek with a kiss. He looked careworn, she thought, as seated at the kitchen table she watched him pour. His hair was thinner now, and grey, and he'd lost his looks. Those ruddy cheeks and broken capillaries round the nose suggested he didn't need the excuse of her first visit for thirty-seven years to open a bottle.

Actually it was far too early for a drink, for her at least. She'd rather have had a cup of tea, but Martin hadn't given her the option. She looked longingly at the kettle. Unlike the door knocker, it shone.

In fact, the whole house smelled of polish, and she was surprised how clean and tidy everything was in here.

'You didn't do all this cleaning for my benefit, I hope,' she said, risking a joke.

Her attempt at humour failed to draw a smile. 'Cleaning? Me? You must be joking.'

He employed a cleaner, he added. She'd not long left, which was why the place smelled so fresh. He seemed annoyed that Carole had turned up in the middle of the day when she could easily have bumped into the woman.

'You know how people talk round here,' he said, tilting his glass towards his lips.

Carole found herself apologising. It was her day off, she said. Dad would be out, and she'd planned to spend the afternoon going through his stuff and chucking out some of the junk he'd accumulated over the years. Martin barely acknowledged her remark. Clearly, what was in his glass was far more interesting.

'Look, Carole. You said you needed to see me urgently. Can we just get on with it, please?' he said when he'd emptied it.

Had he always been like this? So abrupt, so lacking in warmth? She thought perhaps he had. But when you were young, handsome looks and a strong, fit body would generally trump all other considerations. It was only as one got older that one began to put kindness above everything else.

'Adam's back.'

She could have dropped it to him gently. But why should she consider his feelings, since he clearly didn't give a stuff about hers? Her announcement had clearly shaken him. And she was glad. That would teach him to speak to her as if she were his ruddy cleaner. He refilled his glass, tilting the bottle towards her for a refill. She shook her head. Her wine glass was still untouched.

'Tell me,' he said.

So she did. It wasn't easy to get everything out — the photograph of his mother with Lawrence Chambers on the hall table at 5, Marlborough Close; her confrontation with the puppet on the bed and then seeing it again yesterday at the puppet show she'd been hurrying away from when he'd almost run into her as she stepped off the kerb. He kept interrupting her, asking her for details, obviously struggling to piece everything together. Throughout it all, he continued to drink more wine, which only seemed to make him more agitated.

'So you think this is my brother's doing?' Martin demanded when he'd finally processed the information.

'Who else could it be?' she said. 'Who else knows what happened to Lawrence Chambers? No one. Only the three of us.'

He looked down at his glass and swirled the golden liquid round and round. What was he thinking? she wondered. 'I've suddenly remembered that phase he went through when he was a kid, too,' she said. 'The puppet shows, remember?'

'He used to put them on for Dad when he was ill in bed,' Martin said. He finally raised his gaze from his glass. 'Didn't you used to help him make the puppets?'

There was a look of mistrust in his

eyes. Was he accusing her of being in league with Adam? When she had just as much to lose as Martin did, should everything come to light? Carole rose from the table and wandered over to the sink to get a much-needed long, cold glass of water.

'I'm pretty sure he has an accomplice,' she said, turning on the tap. 'Only it's not me.'

'Who is it, then?'

She hesitated. What if she were wrong, and Martin decided to take things into his own hands? He'd done it before, after all.

'Well?' He could barely conceal his irritation. She had no choice now but to speak.

'It can only be George Corker, who runs the estate agent's now,' she said. 'He's the one with the house keys. Not to mention the fact that he sent me to that damn house in the first place.'

'What about the puppet theatre? Did he send you there too?'

There was snarl in Martin's voice. Oh, how she recognised it of old. It was all coming back now. That sense of entitlement. The only damn thing those two brothers had ever had in common apart from their parents. She could almost hear Adam, on those occasions when when she'd ask him to clear his mess away, reminding her that she was 'only' a girl and she couldn't tell him what to do.

'Of course he didn't send me there,' she said. 'It was something my father wanted to do.'

Why did she feel the need to be so defensive? She filled her glass and gulped it nervously, staring out of the window. Down there along the prom, people strolled up and down, enjoying the warm weather and each other's company. Ordinary lives free from fear. Back in Tenerife, that had been her life too. But not any longer.

Her gaze was drawn to a bicycle propped up against one of the outhouses. It was a woman's bike with a huge woven basket at the front. Just as she began wonder where she'd seen it before, Martin spoke again.

'You know what he wants, don't you,

Carole? He wants this house. Well, he can't have it. Mother made it over to me. He ran away and left me to look after her. He can't come slinking back here with his tail between his legs and think he can claim a piece of my legacy just because he's skint.'

This was the other side of Martin. The whining, petulant boy. She must have been mad to get involved with him again. She should have left him to Adam. Left the pair of them to each other.

A sudden breeze tickled the air; a door banged shut. She shivered. It seemed like an omen. She moved away from the window back to the table and exchanged her water for the wine. Raising the glass to her lips, she drained the entire contents. Force of habit from the days when she used to look after Adam sent her back over to the sink to wash it up. It was when she glanced up from the tap that she realised that not only was the bike no longer there, but that she knew where she'd seen it before.

It belonged to Mona. She must have been here — inside the house, while she and Martin had been talking. That ripple of air, the closing of a door. Who else could it have been but her? But what would she have been doing inside Martin's house? Unless . . . Of course! She must be the cleaner Martin mentioned, returning to pick up something of hers she'd left behind. Had she recognised Carole's voice? And what, exactly, had she heard?

★ ★ ★

Laura was enjoying herself. People had remarked on how relaxed she was looking recently. When the super walked past her desk just now, she'd actually enjoyed their little chat. Glancing up from her computer, where she'd been typing up yet one more tedious report, she'd returned his patronising greeting with a wide smile and a thumbs-up.

Yes, sir, she was indeed busy. No, sir, she wasn't overstretching herself. And absolutely, sir, she would definitely make sure she got her break. Off he toddled, satisfied, a big grin on his face, probably thinking he'd gone to sleep and woken up in 1955.

Sleuthing had put the spring back in her step. Perhaps, once her baby had been born and her maternity leave was over, she wouldn't bother coming back as an ordinary DC. Maybe she could set up her own business as a private eye instead. She quite fancied herself in a trench coat and pair of dark glasses. And at least if she were self-employed, she would be able to choose her own cases. Plus, she'd make sure the coffee and biscuits were better quality.

And there was no denying she had a knack for it. Although it wouldn't have taken Sherlock Holmes to make the connection between Carole Prescott and Margot Boulton. The estate agent had been scared witless at the sight of that lookalike puppet, that much was certain. The question now was, why?

The day was still young, and already this morning she'd made great strides. Acting on her hunch, she'd rung Ravi's mum again and asked her if she remembered the name of the girl she'd mentioned who used to help Margot Boulton out from time to time until it transpired she was sleeping with Margot's older son.

Just as Laura had suspected, Mrs Hasheed's memory was razor-sharp. Carole, she said. Carole Prescott. She'd treated her father a few times when he'd still been on his feet and able to come to the surgery where she used to work before her retirement. Carole had been the apple of his eye, apparently, and he was always bringing up her name in conversation, which is why she remembered it so clearly.

'Poor man's had a stroke, I hear,' she said. 'Old age has few comforts, does it, dear?'

Laura liked Mrs Hasheed. She was the perfect interviewee. Told you everything you wanted to know, then wandered off onto a completely different topic without asking you *why* you wanted to know. The opposite of nosy.

She'd also managed a quick glance back through the files pertaining to the mysterious disappearance of Lawrence

Chambers. What struck her most was the fact that no search had been done at the house and no reason had been given as to why not.

The detective heading the case had gone by the name of John Smith. Presumably he'd had his reasons. Or maybe he was just as simple as his name. She made a mental note to find this guy, providing he were still alive and had his marbles, so she could ask him what they'd been.

Her phone rang. It was Will. Had she phoned the estate agent's yet to say they didn't intend putting in an offer for 5, Marlborough Close? Yes, she had, she told him. But she couldn't talk now; she was busy.

'Well, I hope you weren't as short with them as you've been with me,' growled Will before he rang off.

Laura smiled to herself. On the contrary, she'd had a lengthy conversation with Mr Corker. Very informative, too. Especially after they'd got the business of that particular house not being quite right for them out of the way.

'By the way, how's your colleague? The lady who showed us round? I was going to ring her direct line but somehow I've mislaid her number,' she'd said to Corker, crossing her fingers behind her back.

There was a baffled silence on the other end of the line that lasted some time. Finally, George Corker spoke. As far as he knew, Carole was perfectly well. It was her day off today, but she'd be in tomorrow. If Laura preferred to discuss viewing other properties with Carole rather than him, then perhaps she should ring back then.

'Yes,' Laura replied. 'I might just do that. Only, with her fainting the way she did and everything . . . '

'Fainting?'

Laura feigned surprise. 'Oh? Didn't she tell you?'

No, she hadn't. As far as he was concerned, the viewing had gone well. He hadn't had any complaints. Laura reassured him that she was just concerned for Carole and that she certainly wasn't complaining. In fact, she thought Carole had been the consummate professional, she said.

George Corker agreed. 'Carole's been in the business a long time. Started here in fact, then left to work abroad.'

'Oh? When was that?'

More years than he cared to remember, he replied. They'd started off in the same role, both of them school leavers. When she returned to take care of her father a couple of weeks ago, she'd walked in off the street, looking for a job.

'So she's a local girl, then?' Laura said.

Very much so, apparently. Born and brought up in Havensea just like him. In fact, they both went to the same secondary school.

'Oh, which one's that? The Manor or Seacrest?'

He chuckled. 'Good heavens, not Seacrest. Your parents would have to have a bob or two to send you there.'

She apologised. Not being a local, she was still trying to get her head round stuff. 'I guess you'd need to live in one of those big houses along the front to afford those fees,' she said.

He chuckled again. Spot on, he said. The nearest Carole would have come to the uniform of Seacrest was earning a bit of pocket money babysitting for the family who lived up at The White House back then.

Bingo. She'd got what she wanted. Corroboration of evidence she'd already obtained from another source. But even with a missing person, a house unsearched and evidence from Mrs Hasheed that both sons had taken strongly against their mother's new lover, was this enough to take to the super, to persuade him to reopen the case?

She knew the answer without having to ask him. 'I need something more concrete,' he'd say. 'We can't afford to spend money on speculation. This is 2016, Laura, and real life. Not an episode of *Miss Marple*.'

* * *

While she'd been at The White House, Carole had switched off her phone. Now, switching it back on again, she saw she'd had a missed call and a message from George Corker. What the hell did he want on her day off? That one glass of wine had given her a splitting headache. She had enough to think about without adding work into the mix. At least Dad would be at the centre till five, which gave her at least an hour to herself before she started on that clear-out.

George's message was short. He'd sent her an email with a list of all the properties he wanted her to show prospective buyers over the next few days. He hoped she'd be up to it after what had happened at the weekend, he'd said. But either way, he'd be grateful if she'd reply to his email at her earliest convenience.

How the hell did he know about that? she wondered, scrabbling in her bag for her front door key. His next words told her exactly how.

'A Mrs Malone rang, asking after you,' he said. 'She told me about your funny turn. So nice of her to be concerned, don't you think? You obviously made a big impression.'

Carole froze. Mrs Malone. The pregnant one. The copper. Oh yes, she'd made a big impression all right. Big enough for her to go sniffing around asking after her at work. Well, she might have fooled George, but she hadn't fooled Carole. That was no social call. The woman was after her. Sooner or later she'd be round at her front door, asking questions. Just what on earth was Carole going to do then?

Without bothering to take off her jacket, she went straight to her room. The bedroom she slept in now was furnished exactly how it had always been when she'd lived here as a teenager. Her desk was a cheap plywood affair Dad had knocked together for her so she could have somewhere quiet and away from the telly to do her homework. Better to get George's email out of the way right away, she decided, as she went to open her laptop.

But something made her hesitate. She sat there, silent, watchful, both hands flat on the lid of her computer. Something wasn't right, although she couldn't quite put her finger on it. She was almost certain things on her desk had been moved. A drawer she could have sworn she'd left closed was now half-open.

When finally she plucked up courage to open the laptop, she wasn't surprised at what she found. She hadn't logged out before she'd left earlier. Someone had got to George's email before she had.

She thought of that bike, propped up against the outhouse at The White House. She thought of George, and her suspicions about him — suspicions she'd relayed to Martin. It seemed obvious to her that she'd got the wrong culprit. It wasn't George who was in cahoots with Adam Boulton, but Mona Reardon.

She sat there for a long time taking all this in. The house was silent. The only sounds came from outside — passing traffic, seagulls, footsteps. When her doorbell rang, she froze, too terrified to answer. It rang a second time. And then a third. Still she didn't move. Then came the sound of the letterbox being raised and a man's voice calling out her name.

'Carole! Are you there? It's me, George. Please, I wish you'd let me in!'

* * *

Somewhere, hidden behind that huge bouquet, was George. Carole didn't know who she'd been expecting, since one way or another she seemed to be a target for lots of people right now. It wasn't just Adam and Mona who were after her blood. There was that crazy pregnant detective too. It was a total conspiracy!

'I won't keep you,' George said nervously. 'I just wanted to say, first of all, that I hope you're feeling better. And that if you're not up to it, then you mustn't even think about coming in tomorrow. And also . . . '

'You'd better come in,' she said. 'This sounds like it's going to be a long list.'

George smiled, and still clutching the flowers, he stepped inside. When she took the bouquet from him, his hands were shaking. Was she making a mistake inviting him in? The last thing she wanted was to give him the idea that she reciprocated his feelings. At any other time, she'd have left him standing on the doorstep, taken the flowers and pleaded a headache. But right now she couldn't face being alone. And even George's company was better than no company at all. Once he'd gone, she'd have plenty of opportunity to obsess about who'd been reading her private emails and rifling through the contents of her desk.

Once inside the house, she began to hunt around for something to put the flowers in. George followed her from room to room awkwardly, making banal comments about the various features the place had to offer, confirming her worst suspicions. He still fancied her, though the idea of declaring it left him way outside his comfort zone. She was convinced that before too much more time had passed, he'd offer her a valuation on the house instead.

After much vain searching, the only vase she could put her hands on was the old china one with a chip round the lip that had rested on the kitchen table from time immemorial. When Mum was alive, she'd fill it with flowers from the garden in summer and foliage from her walks in winter. When she died, it became a repository for loose change, discarded buttons, anything in fact that hung around the house long enough to be classed as junk. As a teenager, that old vase had been a last resort when it came to raking together the last few coppers to make up whatever deficit she needed for her Saturday night out.

'Anyway,' she said, cutting him off in the middle of a discourse on external wall insulation, 'what's the also?'

Carole tipped out the contents of the vase. A clatter of old keys, foreign coins, dead batteries, curtain hooks and screws of different sizes drowned out her words. There were even a couple of old French francs in there. Useless now, of course.

'I beg your pardon?'

'At the door there. You were apologising. You got to number three on your list.' She took the vase over to the sink and filled it with water, glad of something to do while she waited for George to weigh out his next words.

'Oh. I see.' George's puzzled brow cleared. 'The other thing I wanted to apologise for was bombarding you with work stuff on your day off.'

'I'm fine. Really I am,' she said as during another long silence she busied herself with the flower-arranging.

Perhaps she should offer him a cup of tea, she thought. But that would mean he'd be here even longer. Dad's kettle took an age to boil. What on earth would they talk about while they waited? The wiring, she guessed. She took a step back to inspect her handiwork.

'There,' she said. 'Doesn't that look nice?'

'Very. That must be yours,' he said when her phone bleeped a message.

She glanced at the number through half-closed eyes. When she saw it was one she recognised, she was relieved to be able to put her paranoia on temporary hold.

'Everything okay?' George asked.

'Dad,' she said. 'He forgot to tell me Ollie was meeting the bus that drops him home after an afternoon at the centre.

They're going to The Red Lion for a shandy.'

What a nice gesture of Ollie's, she thought. Dad was always complaining that the centre was full of old folk, most of whom slept through the afternoon. The most exciting thing that had ever happened there, he told her, was when two old ladies got into a fight because one accused the other of cheating at draughts.

'Ollie's dad's carer,' she told George. 'Only a young lad. He's on his gap year and saving up for a ticket to Thailand.'

George tilted his head to one side. 'Ollie?' he said. 'Not Ollie Griffin?'

Carole confessed she didn't know his surname. 'Do you know him then?' she asked.

'Yes. Well, not really. I mean I've met him with his parents once. He was packing his stuff to go and stay with a friend. His parents said they'd never sell the house if he was living there because they couldn't trust him not to destroy the place in their absence.'

George's mention of the name 'Griffin' sparked something in Carole's memory.

Griffin. Griffin. Then it hit her. The Griffins were the couple who owned the house in Marlborough Close. Ollie must be their son!

And that meant he must have a key. He would have been able to slip in at any time of the day or night to plant a photograph or a puppet here. Not only that, but he had access to every room in this house too. To one room in particular. Her bedroom, where she kept her desk and her computer. What had he been looking for?

'Are you okay, Carole?'

Her stomach gave a sudden dreadful lurch.

'I — yes,' she stuttered. 'Only I think perhaps you'd better go, George. I think I'm going to be sick.'

★   ★   ★

Mona had smoked two cigarettes during the time she'd been hovering outside the police station, before she finally overcame her revulsion and went inside. Now she was on her third.

261

She didn't like authority and never had. Right from the moment when her dad had dragged her off to school and the teacher had started laying down the law about which peg to hang her coat on, what desk to sit at, and when she was allowed to go to the toilet, she'd always fought it.

But needs must. She'd examined her conscience and got beyond her initial scruples that she was doing this for the wrong reasons. Namely that she thought Carole Prescott was a bossy cow who needed to be taken down a peg or two. Although fair enough, there was a bit of that involved too if she were honest.

She'd been managing perfectly well looking after old Reg for the last twelve months. Then Miss La-di-da turns up and starts laying down the law. Cheek of it. She'd never had any complaints from the old man himself about her fag habit, had she? And it wasn't as if she was doing it in the house. She'd only ever smoked outside.

But her being here wasn't all about getting her own back on Miss Smarty

Pants. She had a civic duty. She'd heard something she didn't want to hear and wouldn't have heard either if it hadn't been for the fact that she'd left her sunglasses behind at Martin's and gone back to get them.

Between them, those two had been up to something. She might have had weak eyes that watered in strong sunlight, but there was nothing wrong with her hearing. She hadn't caught all of it, but what she had caught had been fraught with urgency. Something about Adam, whoever he was. That he was back and he was threatening to go to the police about them.

What had they been to each other, those two? she wondered. What was their connection with this Adam, and what had they done that was so bad? Taking one last drag of her cigarette, she tossed it on the ground, popped a mint into her mouth and went inside.

★　★　★

Laura had reached a dead end. Detective Inspector John Smith, the officer in charge of the investigation into the death of Lawrence Chambers, had died five years previously. So that was that. Unless someone walked in through the door and plonked a large slice of evidence down on the desk in front of her, she didn't have a leg to stand on.

And speaking of legs, hers were aching like mad today. And her lower back was giving her gyp too. Had she felt like this during her first pregnancy? she wondered. Looking back, she thought she'd rather enjoyed it the first time. Of course, she'd been a few years younger then.

It was the end of her lunch break, and she was taking it alone at her desk because she'd spent so much time on her clandestine investigation that she'd got massively behind in the stuff she was meant to be doing. When her phone rang and she saw Will's name pop up, her mood lifted.

'How are you feeling?'

These were always his first words. He didn't think she should be coming to work at all at this late stage in her pregnancy. But since he couldn't support her in the manner in which she'd like to become accustomed, they really had no choice.

'I'm great,' she said. 'What can I do you for?'

He was just ringing to remind her about the viewing they'd arranged for later that day. Damn, she'd forgotten all about it. Just the thought of tramping round another property and making small talk with the owners made her feel weary.

'Hello? Laura?' Will sighed. 'You'd forgotten, hadn't you?'

She tried to bluff her way out of it, but Will had long ago refined the knack of seeing right through her.

'Tell me if I'm wrong, love,' he said. 'But I can't help thinking you've gone off the boil on this house-move idea.'

'No,' she said, decanting such a large amount of enthusiasm into her tone that she could have been mistaken for a kids' TV presenter. 'Not at all. Just remind me of the address and the time and I'll be there.'

Having taken down the information, she said goodbye. She sat there for a few more minutes, staring at her screen. God, she was tired. If she stayed here any longer, she was convinced she'd fall asleep. What she needed was some fresh air. Just ten minutes and she'd be good for the rest of the afternoon.

But she didn't get that far. Someone was waiting at the desk in the front office. And they wanted to talk to a police officer urgently.

★ ★ ★

'Just what the hell do you think you've been playing at?'

Carole had met her father and Ollie at the door. Dad, well-lubricated with shandy, had been in a buoyant mood. Ollie, perhaps noticing the thin-lipped glare with which Carole assaulted him, appeared more circumspect. Reg had only had one and a half, he assured her, not a pint. As for himself, not a drop of alcohol had passed his lips. Not while he was still on duty.

Dad was in the front room now, flat out in front of the television after his wild

266

afternoon of bingo and his session at The Red Lion. Ollie hovered in the middle of the kitchen, cowering beneath Carole's fierce glare.

'I'm sorry,' he said. 'I didn't think you'd mind. It was such a lovely day. And it was your dad who suggested it, not me.'

He'd worked up a sweat pushing Dad the quarter of a mile from the pub to the house. His long fringe clung to his pale forehead and his nose glistened with perspiration. He was probably in desperate need of a drink of water, but Carole had no intention of offering him one. She would see him crawl across the floor with his tongue hanging out first.

'You still think this is about getting Dad drunk, don't you?' she snapped.

Ollie frowned. His expression was one of a child struggling to work out the answer to a particularly challenging mental arithmetic sum. He looked so young. So vulnerable. Carole was almost beginning to feel sorry for him. But then she remembered what he'd done. Where he'd been. How much he'd terrified her and made her life such a misery over this past week.

'I don't know what you mean,' he stammered.

She gave a hollow laugh. 'Come off it, Ollie. We don't need to discuss what you've been up to. All I want to know is why. How much did he pay you? Adam, I mean?'

A blush crept up Ollie's neck, reaching as far as his ears. He threw his eyes at every surface, unable to meet her harsh gaze. It thrilled her to see how scared he'd suddenly grown. Now he would know how it damn well felt.

'Look,' he said, 'I don't know what any of this is about between you and him. I never even wanted to become involved.'

'Too late for that,' she snapped. 'How did you meet him?'

'I dunno. I can't remember. Some pub. I'd had a drink. I was probably a bit loud. I was telling my friends about work. What I did. I must have mentioned how I came here. You. This house. He came over, bought me a drink. We got talking.'

'And he came up with this little plan.'

Ollie nodded.

'So what were you looking for this time? When you went through everything on my desk?'

'It was stupid of me doing all that stuff. I see it now. It seemed like a laugh at first. Plus, well, you know. I was skint.'

'Answer my question, Ollie.'

His shame rendered his next words practically inaudible. 'He wanted your phone number,' he muttered.

She felt her legs turn to liquid. She willed herself not to show how strongly Ollie's words had affected her. So far, she still had the upper hand, but one false move and he'd soon realise that her bullying manner was simply a bluff.

'And did you give it him?'

'No.'

'Why not?'

He shrugged. 'I don't know.'

'Presumably you have his number on your phone?' she said.

He nodded. She held out her hand and waited for him to root out his mobile from the pocket of his skinny jeans. It was covered in a patina of damp fingerprints.

'It's under Puppet Guy,' Ollie said.

She scrolled down his contact list till she located it. Then she pressed the dial icon. 'By the way,' she said as she waited for it to engage, 'I'll be ringing social services as soon as you've left. Telling them to send someone else from tomorrow.'

'But . . . ' Ollie took a step forward to object, but she cut him off with a warning finger. Adam had begun speaking at the other end. What on earth had got into her? Adam was the last person she wanted to speak to. But somehow it mattered that she kept face in front of Ollie. She had to show him she was someone to be reckoned with. It was almost a relief when she realised it was a recorded message.

The last time she'd heard Adam speak, he was hovering around puberty. His voice had veered between that of a soprano and a tenor, with several scratchy stages in between. Now it was the same pitch as his brother. But somewhere along his life's journey, he'd swapped his public school vowels for something more street. He probably thought he sounded cool, she thought as she listened to his instructions on how to leave a message.

'You wanted my number,' she said when his message came to an end. 'Well, you have it now. And by the way. Tonight. Round seven. I'll be at the White House. We all need to talk.'

She handed Ollie back his phone. He took it from her and squeezed the mobile back into his jeans pocket. Carole held the back door open for him to leave. Meekly, he took the hint. At the door, he turned to face her.

'Can I say goodbye to Reg, before I go?' he said.

She shook her head. She didn't think so, she replied. 'And anyway, it's Mr Prescott to you,' she added.

Ollie looked away, cowed. But then he seemed to regain confidence. 'Just tell me one thing before I go,' he said, raising his eyes to meet hers. 'What did you do to him that made him want to get back at you like this?'

Carole considered his words. A soft evening breeze drifted through the open door. 'Nothing,' she said. 'I did nothing.'

And that was where her guilt lay, she mused as she watched Ollie walk away into the sunset.

★   ★   ★

Laura had made several attempts to locate the super. Nobody seemed to know where he was, and everyone she asked gave her a different opinion as to his suspected whereabouts. She'd come to the conclusion that the most sensible thing to do while she waited for him to return from wherever the hell he'd sloped off to was to jot down in her notebook a list of reasons why he should consider allowing her to pay a visit to Martin Boulton in order to ask him a few questions about the disappearance of Lawrence Chambers, thirty-seven years previously.

If he asked her, she could quote back at him without even looking at it every single lackadaisical bullet point John Smith had made during the six weeks he'd spent on his pitiful investigation. Since her little visit from the woman who turned out not only to be Martin Boulton's cleaner but one of the carers of Carole Prescott's father too, she'd wasted no time doing a bit more investigation into John Smith.

It hadn't taken her long to discover that while he'd been working on the case, two things had happened that might well have taken his mind off the job. First of all, around that time, he'd been nursing his wife, who sadly had died not long after he'd decided to shuffle the file from the top of the pile to the bottom.

Second of all, around that time — presumably because of the pressure he'd been under at home as much as at work — he'd been warned about his drinking. Under a different chief superintendent, he'd have no doubt been taken off the case. She could only surmise that this particular one had felt that to replace Smith with another DI would have felt like he were banging another nail in the poor man's coffin.

But if her own super were unimpressed by that discovery, he surely couldn't fail to agree that Mona Reardon's new testimony was exactly the kind of evidence that called for more serious investigating.

'Who else knows what happened to Lawrence Chambers? No one. Only you and me.' Those were the very words Mona had sworn to Laura that she'd heard. 'I have no idea what it meant,' she'd said. 'But I do know it smells fishy.'

It smelled extremely fishy to her, too. A glance at the clock showed Laura it was already gone six o'clock. Where was he? That ache in her lower back wasn't getting any better sitting on this hard bench outside his office. She hauled herself up and paced for a while, trying to decide what to do next.

Damn this waiting! The whole thing was a no-brainer. She didn't need to talk to the super about what to do next. She was a DI. She could make her own decisions. And what she'd decided was this. She would get in her car, drive herself to The White House, knock on the front door, and speak to Martin Boulton without further ado.

She made her way outside, and

admittedly after a bit of a struggle, strapped herself into her seat and drove off in the direction of Martin Boulton's house.

Back on her desk, her phone beeped an angry message from Will. It was the sixth he'd sent her in as many minutes.

'No point going inside now. Tillie and I are coming home. We've missed the viewing.'

★　★　★

As she watched Ollie walk away, Carole mulled over her situation. But wherever her thoughts led her they always brought her back down the same one-way street. She couldn't get out of this mess, so the only thing to do now was give herself up. She would present herself at the police station and tell them everything she knew about the disappearance of Lawrence Chambers all those years ago. What happened next would be up to them. Quite frankly, it would be a relief to be cut free from this ball and chain of guilt she'd dragged around behind her all these years.

It vaguely crossed her mind that once she'd turned herself in, she'd be putting Martin in the frame. But it had been her misplaced loyalty to him that had put her in this position in the first place. If she'd gone to the police back then and told them what she knew, they'd have arrested him, and she would have been able to walk free for the rest of her life. But as things stood now, she was an accessory after the fact.

Adam too, of course. It suddenly occurred to her he'd be waiting for her at The White House, like he'd promised. What a surprise both brothers would get when the police turned up instead of her.

Dad was still asleep in the front room. She dropped a kiss on his forehead and whispered goodbye. He'd be fine where he was till ten, when Mona was due to pay the last visit of the day and get him ready for bed. Would they let her see him again soon? she wondered as she pulled the door shut behind her. How would she explain it all to him?

It was still light and warm outside. Down on the green, people sat with their friends outside The Red Lion, sharing a drink and enjoying the last of the day's sun. Less than two weeks ago she'd pooh-poohed the idea of Havensea as a delightful resort.

But that was then. At this moment, with the threat of having her liberty snatched away from her, Havensea was indeed the haven by the sea its name proclaimed. She decided to go inside and buy herself one last drink. Prosecco, perhaps. Oddly, considering what she was about to do next, she felt like celebrating. And who knew when she might ever be in a position to drink Prosecco again?

She blinked a few times to accustom herself to the shadowy interior. At first glance, there couldn't have been more than half a dozen people present. Two old men — locals by the look of them — sat by the pinball machine, chewing the fat. A group of pensioners complained about the heat, alternately fanning themselves with menus and sipping their drinks. A tired old dog lapped at the bowl of water that his master, at whose feet he sat, had considerately put out for him.

There was only one person at the bar. He sat with his back to her. From this angle he looked defeated, his shirt stretched tight across his back and his head in his hands. It took her a moment to realise who it was. If only she'd been a little quicker, she could have left without him seeing her. But he must have heard her footsteps as she came in. George.

His expression when he turned round and saw her transformed from one of abject misery into one of happiness. Poor George. It was no use. She was going to have to put him straight once and for all about what kind of woman she was and why it would be totally inadvisable for him to have anything more to do with her. And telling her story would be good practice for when she had to say it all again down at the police station

* * *

Martin was having great trouble trying to keep himself in check as he watched his brother wander round the house, picking up objects and examining them before

278

putting them down again, as if he owned the place. On one occasion he'd practically dropped that Chinese vase of Great-grandfather's, catching it just before it crashed to the ground and smashed into smithereens. He was doing it on purpose, of course. Taunting him, just like he used to do when he was a boy. Was it any wonder he lost his temper the way he did when people goaded him like this?

That damn Lawrence Chambers had been just the same. Kissing his mother in front of him so openly, so lustfully. Watching him over her shoulder while he did so, speaking to him with eyes that said, 'I am the master here now. So you can get back in your box, kiddo, and just remember your place.'

Adam was in the kitchen now, passing comments about all the changes that had been made to the house over the years. He scurried after his brother just in time to see him removing a copper pan from the highest shelf.

'Do you cook much?' Adam removed the lid and stuck his nose inside as if he were sniffing for food.

Martin hovered behind him and waited for him to get to the point. Except he wasn't ever going to get to the point, was he? So it was up to him to do so. 'I know all about what you've been up to, Adam,' he said. 'Carole's told me.'

Adam put the lid back on the pan and set it down on the draining board. *It doesn't damn well live there*, Martin wanted to scream.

'Ah, poor Carole. Still holds a candle for you, does she? Even after everything you've done. Still probably thinks that one day you'll turn into a nice person.'

He turned his face towards Martin and gave a smirk. Martin took a deep breath. He'd had just about enough.

'What do you want, Adam?' he said. 'You promised me you wouldn't come back.'

Adam raised an eyebrow. 'Did I?'

'You know you did.'

'I'm not sure a promise from a boy barely out of short trousers is any more of a promise than one from a dying woman.'

Martin was desperate for a drink now.

But that would mean going to the fridge, and Adam was standing right in front of it.

'Mother left me this house of her own free will. It's written in black and white.'

'Don't make me laugh. You bullied her into it. Like you bullied her into everything,' Adam said. He screwed up his face, and wringing his hands, he declaimed in a manner Martin could only suppose he intended as an imitation of himself, 'Oh, Mummy, Mummy. I don't love you. But if you leave me this house when you die, then I will.'

'Don't be ridiculous,' Martin snapped.

'Ridiculous, am I?' Adam sneered. 'She was terrified of you, Martin. And so was I. Only difference between you and me was that she cared about having your love and I didn't. Not then and not now.'

It occurred to Martin, stupidly perhaps for the first time, that Adam was no longer his little brother. He was — what, forty-eight now? A grown man. One who'd had more than half a lifetime to think about all that had happened back then. Martin was going to have to start thinking himself if he were going to come out best in this duel.

'Mother need never have found out if you hadn't gone and told her what I was planning. I told you in good faith. I thought you were on my side, Adam.' Martin began to shake. 'I did it for us. That man intended to marry her and take this house off us.'

'And as it turned out, he failed at that. Whereas you did rather well out of keeping my half from me.'

'You ran away. You didn't even stay when Mother got ill. It was me who nursed her all those years until she died. I deserved it. And besides, you said you didn't want the house or anything to do with it.'

'I was a kid, Martin. I'd seen what you were capable of. Silencing Mummy, not to mention Carole. She fled the country to get away from you.' He gave a mirthless chuckle. 'Back then, I thought the safest place for me was any place as far away from you as possible.'

Adam turned round to open the fridge door. Martin's breath was coming out in shallow gasps. He felt suddenly impotent. This wasn't how it was meant to go. *He* was the older brother. He had always been in charge.

He saw the copper pan on the draining board, the handle pointing towards him. He heard his brother chuntering on about the contents of the fridge, wondering if he should choose the Sauternes or the Riesling. He smelt the fury in his own nostrils. Then he reached for the pan and brought it down hard on Adam's head again and again and again.

★ ★ ★

Laura had parked her car at the front, thinking the short incline up to The White House could only be good exercise. But by the time she reached the front door, she was struggling to catch her breath, and that lower backache she'd almost forgotten about decided to remind her of its existence again, only this time more persistently.

She rang the bell and waited. It occurred to her that she really ought to let Will know she'd be late. Fortunately, today was his day for the school run, and if she texted him now to remind him of the pasta sauce in the fridge, she was sure he'd have a delicious meal on the table waiting for her when she got home.

She had no intention of dragging this interview out. All she wanted to do was look into Martin Boulton's eyes. Although, she thought her hand buried deep inside her bag for her phone, if she had to wait much longer, she was going to have to assume he wasn't in, in which case she'd be home sooner than she'd anticipated.

Two things occurred to her simultaneously, as she heard footsteps inside. The first was that she'd forgotten all about that damn viewing, and Will was going to be furious with her. The second was that she must have left her phone back at the office.

It had been drummed into her head since the first day of her police training that she must never even think of entering a suspect's premises unless she was able to make contact with a colleague once inside. But when the man she presumed to be Martin Boulton flung open the door and cried out, 'Carole! Thank God you've come!' it was far too good an opportunity to pass up.

He realised his mistake immediately. He stood there, rooted to the spot, his hand on the door, looking her up and down until his eyes came to rest on her stomach.

★   ★   ★

Mona was surprised to get a message from work to tell her she was to take over the entire care of Mr Prescott from tomorrow. When she asked why, the tight-lipped admin assistant on the other end said she didn't know. She immediately phoned Ollie, to see if he was any the wiser.

'I've packed it in,' he said when she asked him what was going on.

She was puzzled. 'But why? You love Reg! And he loves you. His speech and mobility have come on leaps and bounds because of you.'

There was a long silence on the other end. Mona, who had kids of her own and knew a thing or two about them, smelled a rat. 'Just what have you been up to, Ollie? 'Cause none of this sounds right.'

Another long silence. She was beginning to get impatient. But finally everything came tumbling out. And what a garbled account it was too. Something about him taking money off a guy in a pub to leave stuff round his parents' house in order to scare the bejesus out of Carole. What stuff? she asked, trying to make sense of it all. And what was Carole doing at his parents' house? He reminded her they'd got it on the market and Carole was the estate agent showing people round.

'And then she practically caught me red-handed going through the stuff on her desk looking for her mobile number,' he said.

'Why?'

Ollie sighed. To give to this fellow, he said. The one who made him plant the photo and the puppet. This Adam Boulton. And now he felt rotten because he'd lost a job he loved and he'd never see Reg again and he was ashamed of himself. But Mona had stopped listening when she heard the name Boulton.

This had to be something to do with what Carole and Martin had been chatting about yesterday when she'd overheard them talking. Had the police done anything since she'd talked to that pregnant detective yesterday? she wondered.

From the look of the woman, she was about to drop her sprog any minute. Wouldn't surprise her if she'd gone into labour before she'd even written up her statement. In which case, if there were no police officers on the case, somebody else was going to have to sort it out. And that somebody else might as well be her. She wasn't afraid of Martin Boulton just because he lived in a big house.

★   ★   ★

As soon as she was inside, she knew she'd made a mistake. Martin Boulton had taken one look at her ID card before grabbing her by the arm and dragging her into the hallway. How had she got herself into this mess? It would almost be funny if it weren't so terrifying. A man who could bind the wrists and ankles of a pregnant woman and gag her so she couldn't cry out for help was capable of anything.

She just needed to keep a clear head. Will would begin to miss her soon. When he grew tired of being unable to contact her mobile — which he might well already have — he'd ring the station. When she couldn't be located there, they'd mount a search. She'd be home in no time. Except, how would they know where to start looking? Her notebook was still in her bag.

Martin Boulton was pacing up and down in front of her, wild-eyed. She didn't dare look at him in case she panicked him into doing something worse than he already had. She was starting to feel sick and hot and was in desperate need of the loo. *Think of something else*, she told herself, calling on all those sessions of mindfulness she'd done throughout her pregnancy.

She thought she heard a noise. A tap-tap-tapping coming from somewhere else in the house. It grew louder. She heard a groan. Who else was here? she wondered. Then there came another noise. The sound of a key turning in the lock. Footsteps. The door flung open.

'What the hell?'

It was the woman from yesterday. Mona. Was she hallucinating? What was she doing here? But thank God she'd come. In one glimpse she'd seen everything. The terror in her own face, the crazed expression on the face of her captor.

She was suddenly gripped by wrenching cramp that threw her forward. It was pain she recognised from another time — like a belt being pulled tight around her whole lower body. From somewhere within her came a popping sound and then a whoosh of something leaving her body.

'Your waters have broken, love,' said Mona calmly, rolling up her sleeves.

★ ★ ★

She'd given her statement. It had been easy in the end. Martin had confessed to her, and to his brother too, of the murder of Lawrence Chambers in 1980, Carole told the detective inspector. He took it all down without interrupting her, perhaps knowing instinctively that now she'd finally made it this far, she needed to get it all out.

Martin had taken Chambers out on a boat, knowing the man was no sailor. It was Chambers's fault for agreeing to go with him, Martin had insisted. The man was a show-off, always desperate to prove he was the alpha male. Except when it came to sailing, he hadn't got a clue. Which made it the easiest thing in the world to wrong-foot him and tip him over the edge of the boat.

No one missed him, because he'd been a bit of a rogue anyway, involved in all sorts of dodgy dealings, which must have had something to do with the lack of enthusiasm on the part of the police when it came to pursuing their investigations into his disappearance.

George was waiting for her outside

now. He'd told her he'd wait as long as it took, and that meant even if she had to serve time. If that was the case, he said, then he'd visit her till her release, and it went without saying he would personally make sure her father was all right. She believed him. George Corker was a good man, and she'd been foolish for failing to see it.

She'd done nothing wrong by keeping this information away from the police all these years, according to George. Nothing, that was, apart from falling in love with the wrong man. At least she'd had the sense to get away from him as fast as she could once Martin had confessed, he said. She doubted the police would take the same view, but it was comforting to know one person at least had faith in her. The police were on their way to The White House right now. It was finally over.

★   ★   ★

They'd settled on Nichola Mona in the end. Nichola after Will's mum, and Mona after the woman who'd delivered her five minutes before the police came bursting in, putting Martin Boulton in an arm lock and freeing a still-delirious Adam Boulton from the cellar. Two ambulances had arrived shortly afterwards to transport Adam to A&E and Laura to the maternity wing, where she now lay, exhausted but radiant, cradling her new baby girl, with Will and an excited Tillie on either side of her.

'I'm so sorry I forgot the viewing, Will,' said Laura, finally managing to tear her gaze from Nichola's beautiful blue eyes.

'You wouldn't have liked it anyway,' Will said graciously. 'As well as which, I think you ought to save your apologies for the super. Turning up at Boultons' house on your own like that. He didn't like it, you know.'

'Is Mummy in trouble?' Tillie said.

'Under the circumstances, he'll probably decide to be lenient,' Will said, ruffling Tillie's hair.

'What's going to happen to that man who pushed the other man down the cellar stairs?' Tillie wanted to know.

Will and Laura exchanged glances. It had been agreed between them that no mention was to be made about what Martin Boulton had done to Laura. As far as she was concerned, the baby had decided to be born when Mummy was making a routine visit. She seemed satisfied with that explanation.

'I'm sure justice will be done,' Laura said. 'Thankfully, it's no longer any of my business what the courts decide to do with any of them.'

The baby gave a squeak and a snuffle, followed by a wide yawn. They all agreed she was adorable. No one spoke for a long time, so wrapped up were they in the new arrival. It was Will who broke the silence.

'I was wondering, Laura,' he said, his tone tentative. 'Moving house right now. With the new baby and everything. Perhaps we should think about putting it on hold for a while.'

Sometimes she wondered if Will could read her mind. She'd been deliberating on how best to suggest the exact same thing herself.

'That's not actually a bad idea, Will,' she said, stroking the baby's cheek. 'Perhaps we've had enough excitement for a while.'

We do hope that you have enjoyed reading this large print book.

Did you know that all of our titles are available for purchase?

We publish a wide range of high quality large print books including:
Romances, Mysteries, Classics
General Fiction
Non Fiction and Westerns

Special interest titles available in large print are:
The Little Oxford Dictionary
Music Book, Song Book
Hymn Book, Service Book

Also available from us courtesy of Oxford University Press:
Young Readers' Dictionary
(large print edition)
Young Readers' Thesaurus
(large print edition)

For further information or a free brochure, please contact us at:
Ulverscroft Large Print Books Ltd.,
The Green, Bradgate Road, Anstey,
Leicester, LE7 7FU, England.
Tel: (00 44) **0116 236 4325**
Fax: (00 44) **0116 234 0205**

*Other titles in the
Linford Mystery Library:*

COLD CALLING

Geraldine Ryan

Pronounced unfit for frontline duty due to injury, and eligible to retire in a year, DS Fran Phoenix is given a new job heading up the cold cases team — or 'put in a corner' in the basement, as she sees it. Teamed up with a PC with barely two years' experience, they reopen the twenty-five-year-old case of a missing girl — but evidence continues to be thin on the ground. Can the oddly matched duo heat up the trail and uncover the truth? Three stories from the pen of Geraldine Ryan.

LORD JAMES HARRINGTON AND THE CORNISH MYSTERY

Lynn Florkiewicz

While on holiday with his wife Beth in Cornwall, James learns that a local fisherman vanished during the recent opening procession of the Cornish Legends Festival. When more men disappear in broad daylight, he can't help but put his sleuthing hat on. If they were kidnapped, why is there no ransom demand? What are the flashing lights off the coastline? Who is the eccentric woman on the moors? Have the Cornish Legends really come to life? As James delves into the mystery, he realizes his questions come at a price . . .

OUTRAGEOUS SUGGESTION

Ernest Dudley

A woman thinks her plot to murder her husband is foolproof — but it will set off ricocheting complications. When a stranger calls at an old inn during a vicious storm, the elderly resident and her manservant concoct a sinister plan. A travelling salesman picks up a secretly dangerous hitch-hiker. A woman telephones a private detective agency and hangs up abruptly, piquing the curiosity of the investigator. And a knife thrower's assistant is murdered — but is her jealous partner responsible?